Rosemary

The Widows of Wildcat Ridge Series
Book 11

Kristy McCaffrey

ROSEMARY

The Widows of Wildcat Ridge Book #11

Kristy McCaffrey

ROSEMARY

Cover Design: Silver Sage Book Covers
Editor: Mimi The Grammar Chick
Proofreader: Diane Garland

Book Layout © 2019 BookDesignTemplates.com
Typesetting by © Cordially Chris Author Services

E-book ISBN-13: 978-0-9980907-8-8
Print ISBN-13: 978-0-9980907-9-5

https://kmccaffrey.com/
kristy@kristymccaffrey.com

DEDICATION

My gratitude to Charlene Raddon for organizing this series and inviting me to participate, and many thanks to Caroline Clemmons, Linda Carroll-Bradd, Pam Crooks, Tracy Garrett, Christine Sterling, Zina Abbott, and Kit Morgan. It's been a pleasure to work with these talented ladies.

TABLE OF CONTENTS

DESERET NEWS

Salt Lake City, Utah

Est. 1831   Monday, March 31, 1884   Price 10c

Disaster Strikes Gold King Mine

On Friday, March 28, an explosion and fire in the Gold King Mine, Wildcat Ridge, Utah, resulted in a total collapse, killing an estimated 143 miners. Mine owner, Mortimer Crane, says the disaster occurred during the shift change, with men from both shifts being killed. As townspeople attempted to rescue survivors, a second explosion raised the death toll to approximately 175.

Crane states it is impossible to tell now exactly what caused the first explosion and fire or the second explosion. The violence of the blast and faulty shoring is said to have likely caused the lower levels to collapse. Local physician, Dr. Josiah Spense, reported most victims died quickly of suffocation.

Witnesses report that the collapse and explosion were felt as far as thirty miles away. Minor landslides occurred, windows broken and buildings damaged.

Retrieving all the bodies was impossible but a mass burial of those recovered is planned for April 12 at the Wildcat Ridge Cemetery. Anyone wishing to aid the widows and the children left fatherless by the catastrophe may send donations to the Wildcat Ridge Post Office in envelopes marked Donation.

Chapter One

Wildcat Ridge, Utah Territory
August 23, 1884

Rosemary knelt on the ground near her house, digging for the carrots she had planted earlier in the summer. Gardening had offered a sliver of solace after the mining accident at the end of March that had taken the lives of so many men in Wildcat Ridge, including that of her husband, Jack.

She pulled a cluster of medium-sized carrots free and brushed the dirt away with her gloved hand. The raw vegetable smell of wet soil, signaling health and new life, triggered a longing in Rosemary to finally climb from the muck of grief that had consumed her these past months.

"What are you going to do?" Cora asked, blowing a strand of brown hair away from her face as she dug out potato after potato and set them in a basket.

There had been days when Cora Drummond's cheery and irreverent attitude had been the only thing that had moved Rosemary to rise from bed and clothe herself. And just today Rosemary finally had shed the black garments of grieving, wearing a lemon shirtwaist and brown skirt that Jack had chided made her look like a housemaid. His teasing had both humored and irritated her, and how she missed it. She mentally pushed back at the bubble of despair welling up inside her chest.

"I don't know." Rosemary sat on her haunches and wiped her forehead with the back of her hand. It was late afternoon, and the day had been warm. Cora had insisted the garden needed to be plucked, and with so little work for Rosemary at the Assay Office, it was good to feel useful. Cora's husband, Charles, was currently in Salt Lake City trying to set up a new dental practice, so with much spare time, Cora kept many of the widows company, helping where she could.

"Even with the money that Buster gave each of us from the horse sale," Rosemary continued, "and the kind donations from out-of-towners after the mine accident, and the boon from Eleanora's scavenger hunt, I still don't have enough to keep paying the lease on the Assay Office and my home. And Crane is demanding payment by September 1."

"What if you tried to talk to him?" Cora asked. "What if you asked for an extension?"

Rosemary shook her head, trying to suppress her snort of disgust so as not to hurt Cora's feelings. Her friend hadn't been forced into the same desperate situation as the other widows in town—her husband was still alive and well, and she was but a few weeks from joining him in Salt Lake City.

"You are so fanciful, my friend," Rosemary said gently.

Cora surprised Rosemary by laughing. "I suppose I am. I know you're right. Mortimer Crane will bar the door of the Assay Office at midnight on August 31, and by the next day he'll be tearing that building down. But maybe you should ask him anyway? You never know. He might have grown a sliver of compassion that we don't know about."

"Like a wart?" Rosemary smirked. "And you're an eternal optimist. But I do have a plan."

"Well, this is good news," Cora responded, her voice filled with the kind of praise a parent reserved for a child who had done well on their homework. There were times when Cora seemed far older at twenty-five, despite Rosemary being only four years younger.

"Jack was always talking about the Old Spanish Mines that were supposedly in this area. He and I both loved geology, and he would often go traipsing around in the countryside. Sometimes I would accompany him, but often he would go alone. He did like his solitude." Sadness bubbled to the surface.

Five months. Jack had been gone only five months. It felt like a lifetime.

Rosemary cleared her throat. She had been stuck in limbo all summer long, unable to decide about anything. But not anymore.

"There was one mine in particular that fascinated him," she continued. "It was called The Floriana. He'd been sure he was closing in on the location and had even done some preliminary testing. But then winter came, and travel became limited. And then …"

The accident.

She paused again, blinking back tears.

"It won't always be so hard." Cora's soft tone was filled with compassion.

Rosemary nodded, a bit too vigorously. "I suppose not."

But as much as Rosemary adored Cora and cherished their friendship, her friend hadn't lost a husband on that fateful March day. She couldn't truly understand. But maybe that was why Rosemary had leaned on Cora more than ever during this difficult time. The other widows had been juggling equal amounts of grief, desperation, and relief. Not all marriages had been happy ones. But Rosemary had loved Jack, and although they'd been married only a short time, she was still reeling from the loss.

She took a steadying breath. "I'm going to find The Floriana Mine."

Cora froze. "In the hills? Alone?"

"I don't have a choice."

"What if it's just a rumor? A silly story to drive prospectors mad with gold fever?"

"But what if it's true? Look at what Braxton Gamble found." During the summer, before he had married Priscilla Heartsel, who had lost both a husband and a father in the mine explosion, Braxton had stumbled across an old and very promising Spanish mine in the hills south of town. He was currently in the process of getting it up and running.

Rosemary continued in a rush, as much to convince herself as Cora. "If I can locate something—anything—of merit out there, then I can test the ore samples myself. If they're good, then I would contract an independent assay out of Salt Lake City. I have a tiny bit of money set aside for that. This might entice an investor to buy the claim. This could give me leverage with Crane to keep Jack's business—my business—as well as my home. I really want to remain in Wildcat Ridge. And if I had enough money, I could repay the kindnesses that so many of the widows in town have extended to me."

"Oh, Rosemary, you know that no one expects repayment. And I hate to be a curmudgeon, but Crane has insisted that your husband run your business. Even if you can continue paying the lease, what about that stipulation?"

Rosemary released a frustrated huff, a few foul words that she'd heard Jack utter on the tip of her tongue. Mortimer Crane was a cockroach. "First things first. If I can wave the promise of money under his nose, I'm hopeful that this 'husband' situation can be overruled."

"You mean run the Assay Office yourself? Without a man?"

"I've been doing it all summer anyway. My father taught me to assay when I was young. I instructed Jack in the beginning before he got the hang of it. So why shouldn't I run the business? I don't need or want to marry, except for this financial issue that's hanging over me like a black cloud. And besides, you know I loved Jack. I can't imagine being with anyone else."

Doubt shadowed Cora's gaze. Rosemary couldn't fault her. Convincing Crane to renew her lease without the promise of a man taking over was likely nigh to impossible. Still, she had to try. But first, she needed a windfall of credit to make it happen.

Cora chewed her lip. "I really don't think you should go alone into the hills. With Mr. Gamble working his new mine, all sorts of questionable characters have been seen around town." She wrinkled her nose. "They certainly don't bathe often enough, and besides that, I fear many aren't gentlemen. And haven't some of them come to you for an assay?"

"Some. Most of them don't like the fact that a woman is doing the testing. They're all running to that fella in Cranesville. I think his name is Frankie Edwards. Jack was acquainted with him."

"Well, exactly."

Confused by Cora's response, Rosemary frowned at her friend.

"I don't think you should be running around the hills alone with these types of men loose," Cora clarified.

"I traveled with Papa on his surveys all the time." Rosemary stood and dusted the dirt from her skirt, just as she wished to flick away her guilt over the estrangement from her father. But how could she forgive him after the lies he had told her about her mother? She picked up the basket of carrots and carried them to the house porch, setting them on the stoop. "I'll be fine."

Cora deposited her bounty beside Rosemary's. "I should go with you," she said. "Can you wait a few days? Martha isn't feeling well, and I promised Doc Spense that I'd help in his office, at least until the middle of the week."

Rosemary flicked her blond braid from her shoulder. "I don't want to wait any longer. I still have Jack's six-shooter, and I know how to use it. I just need to borrow a horse and get some supplies."

Cora planted her hands on her hips. "All right. I can see you've made up your mind. Buster might have a horse she could loan you. I think she's got a few at the livery. Maybe you could ask her tomorrow at church. And I could gather some food for you. How long will you be gone?"

"I really think I could do this in two days. Maybe three."

"What if you get lost?"

"Jack was very detailed in his descriptions, and he kept a notebook with his observations. I'll use it as a reference. I know this is a longshot, but I have to try."

"I suppose. But if you find nothing, then please return quickly. And it's not the end of the world if you lose the Assay Office. If you lose this place—" she gave a nod toward the small house "—then you can come live with me. And you can even come to Salt Lake City when I join Charles. You don't have to stay here.

"I know, but it's my home." *And Jack is buried in the cemetery.* He was one of the few to have a headstone and a proper resting place. Unfortunately, many of the remains had been impossible to identify.

But if Crane took her business, Rosemary knew that she wouldn't be able to stay. She could certainly take up Cora's offer, but she didn't want to. Her only other option would be to contact her father, but that was the last thing she wanted to do. Although she hadn't seen in him in over three years, she had heard from her Aunt Louisa that he hadn't approved of Rosemary's hasty marriage to Jack, or of Jack himself. And he had conveyed his displeasure that his only daughter would move to the middle of nowhere in the Utah Territory.

But Rosemary hadn't just fallen in love with Jack; she had also found a connection to the people and locale of Wildcat Ridge. The wilderness was a balm to her soul, and despite the hardships that she and Jack, and many others, had endured to eke out a living here, she had found a place that called to something deep inside her. And even more so now. The tragic loss of so many men—including her own love—had prompted many townsfolk to leave. But with those who had stayed, Rosemary felt an especially close kinship.

They were surviving.

She wasn't ready to give up yet.

"All right then," Cora said, her tone decisive. "Let's get you ready for your adventure."

Chapter Two

August 29, 1884

As soon as Miles McGinty entered the outskirts of Wildcat Ridge, people stared. And all were women.

He supposed the town was small enough that a stranger riding in would cause a stir of interest, and he did his best to smile and tip his hat as his horse trotted down Front Street, but after the thirtieth time he'd done it he began to wonder two things: Had his mama forgotten to tell him he was so homely as to draw unwarranted attention? Or was the opposite true, and had he suddenly become irresistible to those of the female persuasion?

He suppressed a grin at both thoughts. He was likely somewhere in the middle. These ladies must simply know the comings and goings of every man, woman, and child in town, so he was currently sticking out like a sore thumb.

As he rode and scanned the buildings, he did

his best to ignore the scrutiny. When he came to a cross street, he turned to the right, guessing that the business he sought would be located near the abandoned mine in town. And it was. On the corner of the next street over was the Assay Office.

He dismounted, looped the reins of his horse, Pearl, on the hitching rail, and knocked his Stetson up a notch so that he could see better.

A CLOSED sign hung in the window.

Now what?

He glanced around. A woman with brown hair and a curious gaze watched him from the bridge across the creek. He gave a nod and approached her.

"Pardon me, ma'am." He removed his hat. "I was wondering if you'd know when the Assay Office would be open?"

She eyed him with wariness and a bit of curiosity. "I'm not sure. Do you have a sample that needs testing?"

"No. I'm looking for Rosemary Brennan."

"Are you a friend?" She fiddled with the closed parasol in her hand.

"Of a sort. I knew her husband, Jack. I corresponded with Mrs. Brennan after the terrible accident and told her I'd be coming for a visit to pay my respects. And to meet her."

The woman's eyes softened as he spoke, so he also added, "I was very sad to hear that Jack had died." His throat tightened, straining his voice. He hadn't thought his arrival in town would get to him, but apparently, he was wrong. "Did you know him?"

The woman nodded. "I did." She extended her hand. "I'm Mrs. Drummond. Cora Drummond."

He shook it.

"Rosemary never said anything about your letter," she continued, squinting at him.

"Is she here?"

The woman went silent, her gaze taking his measure. "Were you a good friend of Jack's?"

"He was like a brother to me." Again, he could barely squeeze the words out. He rubbed a hand at the back of his neck to shake the stark loss of Jack. Except that Jack's real name was Johnny Briggs. But Miles doubted anyone here knew that. Johnny had wanted a fresh start, and Miles had been quietly supportive. He'd had a chance to help a young man in a way he hadn't been able to with his own brother, Billy.

"Where have you come from?" Mrs. Drummond asked.

"Oklahoma Territory."

"What profession are you in that allows you to leave for a period of time?"

She was sizing him up, wondering if he were trustworthy. In a way, it warmed his heart that Jack had found a place with friends such as this.

"Up until two years ago, I was a U.S. Deputy Marshal. But once that ended, I settled into carpentry. I guess I've got a bit of a wanderer's soul in me, so I'd planned to visit Jack earlier this year but was waiting for the weather to break. And then, I heard of the accident. I debated whether to come—I don't want to be a bother to his wife—but it would mean a lot to tell her how sorry I am that Jack is gone."

Mrs. Drummond paused, then gave a cursory look around her before saying in a low voice, "I'm worried."

"About Mrs. Brennan?"

The woman nodded. Speaking quickly, she said, "Rosemary has gone into the hills to look for gold. She needs money, you see. Mortimer Crane, who owns much of this town as well as the mine that exploded, is set to turn her out come August 31."

"She's looking for gold to pay her debt?"

"Yes. She was planning to head out on Sunday but then had to wait on a horse, so she departed town on Monday. She was supposed to return a few days later, but now it's Friday." She stopped and took a deep breath.

"You think something has happened?"

"I don't know. She didn't want me to say anything. There are a lot of prospectors around who would be quite happy to take anything she found. But I'm on the verge of going to our town marshal, Cordelia Wentz."

"I'll tell you what. I'll see if I can find her. Can you give me some idea in which direction she went?"

She nodded. "I can tell you generally, but I really don't know the exact location." Her voice rose in distress.

"Don't worry. I have skills in tracking. Would anyone know about the horse she took?"

"Yes, Buster loaned her one. Or rather, Mrs. Blessing King. You could go talk to her. She and her husband run the Rafter O Ranch just north of Wildcat Ridge."

Miles began to think of the supplies he would need. "Is there a mercantile in town?"

"Yes." She pointed behind her. "Tweedie's is right there."

"Good. I'll grab a few supplies. Then can you take me to see this Mrs. King?"

She gave a nod.

"And may I ask you something?"

"What's that?"

"Why was everyone staring at me when I rode into town?"

For the first time, Mrs. Drummond's face lost its worried expression. "Oh, that. Are you married?"

"No."

A brief smile flashed across her face. "Would you like to be?"

Chapter Three

August 30, 1884

Rosemary peered through a large bush at the two unkempt men sitting just beyond. Shivering from the late afternoon chill, she pulled her duster more tightly around her and glanced up at the foreboding clouds gathering, blue sky quickly losing ground to gray thunderclouds.

Her time in the hills had produced a few promising clues as to the whereabouts of The Floriana Mine, along with a handful of samples she wanted to test. This had buoyed her flagging spirits, because she had quickly become overwhelmed by the wild and vast backcountry. She had relied on Jack during their time spent in the wilderness, and it was clear now how much she had leaned on him.

To worsen matters, yesterday she'd lost Madge, the horse that Buster had loaned her. Her run of bad luck had started when she'd fed the animal a carefully measured portion of oats, and when more wasn't quickly forthcoming—supplies needing to be rationed—the contrary beast had bitten Rosemary on the neck just below the ear. The ensuing melee between woman and horse had caused Madge to bolt.

Rosemary grimaced from the discomfort of the wound, although thankfully there had been little blood. It was more the guilt she felt that pained her. Heartbroken over losing the animal, Rosemary had frantically searched for her. Not only had she not located the horse, but she had become so disoriented that she was now well and truly lost.

She hoped Madge, despite being a mite temperamental, would be all right, and Rosemary added a silent prayer that she still might locate her. Rosemary's heart squeezed, not just for the horse but for having to tell Buster that she'd been so stupid as to lose the critter, not to mention that her samples were in the saddlebags. On the horse.

She had been overly confident in her abilities, that was certain. Her father had taught her surveying, and Jack had taught her how to read the land, but she had not been out on her own. All night, she had ruminated over where she might have gone wrong, but the truth was that it had been shockingly easy to lose her focus in her frantic bid to find Madge. Only too late Rosemary had realized her error.

Taking a steadying breath, she willed her frantic thoughts into submission.

It's only been one day since I became lost. Madge must be around here somewhere. And while Rosemary was cold and hungry, she just needed a little help. And stumbling across these two men was a possible answer to her silent pleas to the Good Lord upstairs.

And yet, she held back from approaching them. They were clearly prospectors. She had met such men while assisting Jack in the Assay Office, and while most weren't the bad sort, some niggle of doubt kept her from leaving the safety of her shrub.

I fear many aren't gentlemen.

Cora's words echoed in her ears. But Rosemary had no choice. No one would come looking for her. Even if Cora went to Marshal Wentz for help, she really had no idea where Rosemary had gone.

It had been foolish to come out here. But what choice had she had?

Before she could talk herself out of it, she left her hiding place. Cognizant of not having the six-shooter—that, too, was with the horse—she walked slowly forward, ready to run if need be.

One of the men caught sight of her. "What the …"

He pushed to his feet, and then his friend did the same. Although both appeared to have been living in the wilderness for quite some time, upon closer inspection they were both younger than Rosemary had assumed. More alarm bells went off in her head, but she forged ahead with her intention of asking for help.

"Good afternoon," she said. "I wondered if I might trouble you gentlemen for some aid. I've lost my horse and have become disoriented myself. I need to return to Wildcat Ridge. Would you know how far away that is? And in which direction?"

The first prospector frowned, his eyes squinting in suspicion. "Who are you?" he asked, his bedraggled beard bobbing as he spoke.

She hesitated, wanting to share as little information as possible, but couldn't think of a suitable fabrication. "Rosemary Brennan."

When the prospector's eyes widened with recognition, she halted her forward movement.

I should have lied.

But it was too late.

"Your husband ran the Assay Office," the man said, pointing a finger smeared with dirt in her direction. "Jeremiah. No, that's not it. Jacob?" He turned to his friend. "What was his name?"

His friend, wearing a hat splotched with dirt and sweat, eyed her with a calculating scan. "Jack."

"That's it. That no-good, rotten scoundrel doctored reports."

Rosemary gasped. "He did not. How dare you accuse him?"

The other prospector threw a surprised glance at his partner. "Is that so?"

"Didn't I tell you?" the bearded one asked. He huffed. "Well, it's true. 'Course it's true." He returned his attention to Rosemary. "Why are you out here?" A dawning realization ignited his eyes. "Are you scouting claims? Is he letting his wife run around stealing plats?"

Rosemary squared her shoulders, outrage filling her with a resolve she'd not experienced since losing Jack. "If you must know, my husband is deceased. And he was no thief, and neither am I."

"Did he die in that godawful mining accident? We'd heard the Assay Office was still open, but there was no way in hell I was stepping foot in there again." The prospector's voice rose with every angry word he spit out. "Had three good samples I took him, and they all came up empty."

"Sometimes you just have a bad sample," she said. "It could very well have been that you had a good claim."

"Well, I never filed based on those reports, and now that land is gone."

"Who claimed it?" she asked.

"Mortimer Crane."

Why would Crane stake a claim when Jack's assays had showed the land to be worthless?

Conflicted about her husband possibly contributing to the underhanded deeds of the loathsome Mortimer Crane, while at the same time needing help from these prospectors who possibly were just as underhanded, she blurted, "I could run new samples for you at no charge. In exchange, all I ask is that you help me."

"We don't want nothin' to do with you." Bedraggled beard shifted a bulge in his cheek and spit brown tobacco juice onto the ground.

For a moment, Rosemary stood rooted in place. It was clear these men wouldn't help her, and frankly, she didn't want them to. But she couldn't keep wandering the countryside. With a storm threatening, the ensuing cold spell could put her in more dire circumstances soon if these men abandoned her.

"Please, I need help. I can't find my way back to town."

"You shoulda thought of that before you came out here," the bearded one replied. "This is no life for a woman."

"Hey, Alvin," filthy hat said, eyeing her up and down.

The back of Rosemary's neck tingled. *Run. Just run.*

She took a step back, and then another.

"What if we keep her?" the other one said.

"Why in God's name would we do that, Hector?"

"We could ransom her to Crane."

Alvin stared at the other man. "Are you out of yer ever-lovin' mind? We could go to jail for that. And why would Crane even want her?"

"Because she's falsifying reports for him too, just like her dead husband."

Rosemary didn't bother to defend herself, knowing her refutations would be useless. Instead, she continued moving backwards, one tiny step at a time.

Hector spied her retreat and walked quickly toward her.

She turned and took off running.

Fear gave her a burst of energy, briefly staving off her weakened state. Lifting her skirt, she moved downhill and through a copse of pines, but her petticoats caught on a fallen log and she tripped, flying face forward and hitting the ground hard.

Stunned, she struggled to breathe. A glance back showed Hector in swift pursuit.

Shocked by his speed, she pushed upright and resumed her scramble to escape. As she came around a thicket, she nearly slammed into her horse.

"Oh, Madge! Thank the Maker!"

The horse nickered and danced in nervousness. Rosemary ran a hand along her neck, reassured that the animal appeared unhurt. She quickly retrieved her six-shooter and readied it.

She heard a loud thump and a scuffle.

With the weapon raised, she backtracked her escape path.

Two men rolled in the dirt, locked together like battling bull elk. Another horse stood vigil, minus its rider, who must be the man currently fighting Hector on her behalf. For a split second, she thought it might have been Priscilla's husband, Braxton, but the man grunting and, unfortunately, losing ground to the likes of Hector, was a stranger to her.

Friend or foe, she couldn't let Hector win.

"Freeze or I'll shoot," she said loudly.

Both men stopped and looked at her.

"Who are you?" she demanded of the stranger.

"McGinty," he wheezed past the chokehold Hector had on him.

McGinty? That sounded familiar.

"Let him go, Hector," she demanded, "before I drag you to the marshal and have you locked up."

A wicked grin spread across Hector's face. "How you gonna do that? You're as lost as a whore in church."

Rosemary inhaled sharply. "You're a despicable human being, and if you don't release Mr. McGinty right now, I'll shoot your foot off."

Hector chuckled and gripped his arm tighter around McGinty's neck. The stranger's face was starting to turn purple.

Rosemary cocked the gun and closed her right eye to line up the sight with her left the way she had practiced with Jack. Without hesitation she fired, the kick from the weapon knocking her backwards with a scream. As she scrambled to her feet, Hector was howling, but Mr. McGinty had managed to free himself.

Alvin ran toward them with a lopsided gait, huffing and sweating. He might be young, but he acted like an old man.

Mr. McGinty grabbed a shotgun from his horse and aimed the firearm at the two prospectors.

"She shot me!" Hector wailed.

Rosemary remained where she was, a terrible trembling overcoming her. *Good Lord, I did shoot him.*

Alvin bent down to examine his friend's leg, wheezing as he spoke. "Now, Hector, she barely grazed you."

"She shot my foot off!"

Alvin shook his head, his mouth buried in the mop of whiskers that hung from his chin. "Nope. The bullet's in the ground, not yer foot. She made a hole in your trousers, that's all. I see a tiny speck of blood, but I'm not sure since you're a mite filthy."

"Grab her!" Hector insisted. "We'll take her to Wildcat Ridge and have her arrested."

"I don't think so," Mr. McGinty finally chimed

in. "You were chasing *her*. What did you plan to do when you caught her?"

Hector's expression turned incredulous. "Who the blazes are you? And how do you know she's not my wife? Or somethin'?"

Mr. McGinty looked at her and the full brunt of his attention stilled her breath. Before she turned purple herself, she gulped air into her lungs. He was tall and strong and … how on earth did the likes of Hector best this man?

"Are you his wife?" he asked. "Or somethin'?"

She didn't miss the flash of amusement in his eyes before he flicked his gaze back to the two prospectors.

"I most certainly am not his wife," she answered, her voice shaky. She placed the gun in her coat pocket, and then wrung her hands together. She'd never shot a man before, and she didn't much care for it.

Hector stood, clearly none the worse for wear, except he looked irritated that he could stand on both of his legs. "Well, I'm pressing charges against you." He pointed at Mr. McGinty.

McGinty's brows raised in surprise. "For what?"

Rosemary caught herself staring at the stranger's

rugged profile. He'd lost his hat in the scuffle. His dark hair was short and mussed, and his chin was sporting a dark stubble.

"You were chasing a defenseless woman," McGinty continued. "I could have *you* arrested."

Alvin puffed his chest and held a hand up to McGinty. "All right, all right. This was all just a huge misunderstandin'. How's about we call it even and go about our business?"

"It's up to her." McGinty angled his head in her direction.

Still trying to get her nerves under control, Rosemary wanted nothing more than to be rid of Alvin and the especially vile Hector. But her only option was this stranger. Was she trading one bad situation for another?

"I'm needing help in returning to Wildcat Ridge," she said to her rescuer. "Might I prevail on you to help me? I'd just as soon never see these two lowlifes again."

McGinty gave a nod, then waved his shotgun at the two men. "Get lost."

The two men loped away. When they were out of view, McGinty lowered his firearm and approached her.

"Are you Rosemary Brennan?"

She nodded, noticing that his brown eyes held a hint of amber as he came closer.

He held out a hand. "I'm Miles McGinty, Jack's friend."

"Oh." She clasped his palm, warmth spreading from her fingers into her belly. She had exchanged a letter with him after Jack's death. "How did you find me?"

He released her. "A Mrs. Drummond was concerned and told me how to find you."

"She did?"

His hard features softened. "Not really. She gave me a general direction, but it took some serious tracking to find you. You're far from town. Did you know that?"

Her shoulders sagged. "Yes. I'm lost. Thank you for your help with those … men."

He ran his fingers through his hair, and having retrieved his hat, settled it into place. "I think I have to thank *you*. Where did you learn to shoot?"

"Jack."

He nodded. "My thanks for not shooting *me*." A slight smile tugged at his lips.

Comprehension washed through her. "Oh my

…." Her hand came to her chest. "I'm so terribly sorry. I could have hurt you. I don't know what I was thinking. Jack taught me to shoot bottles, not people." Her throat tightened and tears rushed to her eyes.

"Easy." McGinty rested his hands on her shoulders. "Hector was scrappier than I'd anticipated. You did the right thing."

She cleared her throat. "Well, yes, I did wonder how he was able to get a hold of you. You're so"— her gaze skimmed his shoulders—"wide."

He removed his hands. "Maybe we can keep the Hector incident between us."

She flashed him a look of confusion.

"I didn't mean we should let him get away with trying to hurt you. If you want to press charges, I'll be the first to back you up. It was a jest. I'll even confess to the fact that you saved me."

That made her laugh, which honestly felt good. The past day had been a trial. "I hardly think you needed saving, but you're welcome. I remember your letter. I'm so sorry that I didn't realize that you'd be coming to visit Jack's grave."

"I apologize for dropping in unannounced, but I was able to get here sooner than expected."

"Well, I'll be forever grateful that you did."

"We won't be able to make it back to town before nightfall, but if we get started, we can cover a bit of ground before it's too dark. We should be back by tomorrow, late morning."

She nodded, then glanced around for her horse. "Madge got away from me yesterday, so the poor thing has been saddled all night."

McGinty walked with her to retrieve both his horse and Madge, then he helped her feed the animal. They removed the saddle and brushed her, and he led both horses to a stream to drink.

"I think she'll be fine to ride," he said. "We'll give her a good rest tonight when we stop."

Rosemary would be sleeping under the stars with a strange man and no chaperone. She should be shocked and mortified, but she wasn't. She was a widow. She was no naïve maiden. And she'd barely avoided whatever may have occurred at the hands of Hector. The thought sent a shiver through her.

If townsfolk gossiped about her and McGinty, then let them. He had helped her. He was Jack's friend, and truthfully, it would be nice to catch up with him, to be with someone who had known her husband, someone who might feel a sliver of the grief she felt from losing Jack Brennan.

McGinty saddled Madge again and helped Rosemary onto the animal, and then he began leading her home.

Chapter Four

McGinty settled the horses for the night and then joined Rosemary at the campfire she had built. The threatening storm had miraculously passed, revealing a pitch-black sky filled with twinkling dots. It would be cold tonight, and Miles had an extra blanket he would offer to Mrs. Brennan, but he resigned himself to keeping the fire going until morning.

He surveyed the perimeter once again. He didn't think Hector and Alvin would pursue them, but when it came to some men, one never knew.

Despite Rosemary looking exhausted after the night without her horse, there was no doubting her beauty. Jack hadn't embellished that fact in the letters he'd sent to Miles. And such a thing might twist a man like Hector into taking bold—and dangerous—chances.

Miles sat across from Rosemary, and she handed

him a plate of food—bread and beans—which he gratefully accepted.

"Not quite how I anticipated our visit," he said.

"I can't believe I got lost. Usually I'm better at keeping track of landmarks and distances."

"Why are you out here?"

She sighed. "It's a long story and not one to trouble you with. I'm happy that you've come. Jack spoke very highly of you, and I'm so sorry that we couldn't have met under better circumstances."

Miles scooped the last of the beans into his mouth and set down the plate. "I still can't believe he's gone. You said he was in the mine when it collapsed?"

Rosemary nodded. "He'd gone to gather a sample for the mine owner, a man named Mortimer Crane, and …" She paused, and then plastered a stalwart smile on her face. "It was really bad timing. Jack wasn't the only man lost. There were so many …." She stared into the fire. "Such a terrible tragedy."

"I'm surprised you've stayed."

"I like it here. And Jack's here. I'm able to place flowers on his grave every week. That gives me some measure of comfort."

"I'd be pleased to accompany you on one of those visits."

"Of course," she replied. "There's a nice boardinghouse in town, very near my house. You can stay as long as you like. In fact, Mrs. Loftin would probably give you a discount for an extended stay."

Her earnest invitation stirred something in his heart. He had never really put down roots. Maybe staying for a spell would do him good. "I'd like that," he said with genuine intent. "When I met Jack in the Oklahoma Territory, I never thought he would move west. Did he like it here?"

Having finished her food, Rosemary brushed her skirt free of crumbs. "Oklahoma?" Her brows furrowed. "Jack said he met you in Kansas."

And in that moment, the truth sank in. Jack had never revealed his criminal past to his wife. "Yeah, Kansas. Sorry. Slip of the tongue."

She smiled. "He said you were a U.S. Deputy Marshal. You probably have many stories to tell. It's no doubt easy to get them all confused."

Lying to her filled him with unease, but he could well imagine why Jack hadn't told her. It wasn't Miles' place to override that decision even though Jack was gone. The pain of that loss still felt as raw as when he had learned of Jack's death.

While deception had sometimes been necessary in his line of work—most notably his time with Jack's gang—Miles' head and heart raced over whether to tell Rosemary the truth.

He leaned forward and said, "How did Jack describe the first time he and I met?"

"He said that he was caught up in a bank robbery."

Maybe he *had* told his wife. "He admitted ..."

"He had been in the bank, minding his own business, waiting for the teller to be free, when several armed men entered. You saved the day, and you and he became friends."

He sighed. It was probably best to say very little. He would leave Wildcat Ridge soon enough, and he didn't want to ruin Rosemary's memories of her husband.

"Yeah, that was it," he said quietly.

"Jack always said you were like the brother he never had."

Another lie. Everett "Shady" Briggs was Jack's brother. It was Shady that Miles had been after when he had infiltrated Jack's gang.

"I felt the same," Miles replied, and it was true.

Jack had saved Miles' life, causing a permanent rift with Shady and the necessity of a new start. One that Jack had begun with Rosemary.

"He did mention that you had lost your own brother," Rosemary said, her voice quiet and sympathetic. "I'm so very sorry."

Miles' chest tightened. His younger brother, Billy, had been unruly and smart-mouthed, and stubborn to a fault. When he'd gotten himself mixed up with Shady Briggs, the result had been devastating. Briggs had gunned Billy down during an argument over stolen horses, and for that Miles had pursued Shady with the single-minded intention of bringing him to justice and locking him away for a lifetime. But then Miles' cover had been blown, and he'd only survived—and escaped—with Jack's help. During his recovery he'd ended his tenure as a U.S. Deputy Marshal, and with Briggs disappearing, Miles had sought to quiet the need to chase the man to the ends of the earth. Easier said than done, but these days Miles was striving for a life of substance over vengeance. He wanted more of the things that mattered—family and friendship. Maybe even love.

He glanced at Jack's widow, her eyes haunted with grief, and the need to comfort her was strong.

Telling Rosemary some version of the story of Billy's death would require too much distortion of the facts, and he didn't have the heart to continue misleading her, so he simply nodded and passed on further explanation.

"Was Jack happy in Wildcat Ridge?" he asked.

"Yes." Pain and love crossed her face. "At least, I think so. When we married, he said he was ready for a fresh start, and so was I. So we picked up and left Kansas. Jack had been learning how to assay and he quickly found work here. The man who runs the town—Mortimer Crane—liked Jack and hired him right away to work in the Assay Office."

"And you're still running it?"

"I am. Well, I'm trying to. There's not been much business over the summer, what with so many men lost and the mine closing. And then Crane moved his operations to a new town called Cranesville. Guess who it's named after?" She grimaced.

"I take it you don't like this Crane fella."

She gazed into the fire, the orange glow illuminating a face that reminded him that beauty still existed in the world. "I don't. And Jack was really at the man's beck and call. It annoyed me at times. But he paid well, and we had a lovely home, so it was certainly not right for me to complain. But … Jack shouldn't have been at the mine that day. I suppose I'll always blame Crane for that."

"Maybe you should leave Wildcat Ridge."

She tugged the blanket tighter around her shoulders. "Of course, I've considered that. Many women did go, but many have stayed. Despite Crane and the dreadful memories that haunt the widows, I like it here. There's a freedom to this land that I've never experienced anywhere else. I just …." She paused.

He smiled and placed more wood onto the fire. "You've found your bliss."

"My what?"

He poked at the wood, sending a flurry of orange sparks upward. "You've found a place that makes you more of yourself rather than less."

She was silent for a moment. "That's a nice explanation. I suppose you're right."

"What were you looking for out here?"

"Jack had been searching for an old Spanish mine called The Floriana." She shrugged and smiled. "I decided to come looking for it."

"Did you find it?"

"No. These hills don't give up their secrets

easily."

Neither do men.

Chapter Five

August 31, 1884

As they neared Wildcat Ridge, Rosemary gained her bearings once again. She didn't feel much like riding straight through town, since her bedraggled appearance would undoubtedly cause a stir. She would need to explain where she'd been and why she was currently in the company of a handsome stranger. Added to that was the accusation from Alvin regarding Jack's possible collusion with Crane by falsifying assay reports. She needed time to process this.

But then she remembered that today was Sunday, and a quick glance at the pocket watch she kept with her told her that she was currently missing church. She praised her good timing.

She led McGinty down a mostly empty Chestnut Street and straight to her house.

She could feign illness for missing services and

keep her excursion into the hills to herself. Cora had said she would keep an eye on her house while she was gone, and with hope Hester Fugit—Rosemary's closest neighbor and the mayor—had been too busy to notice that Rosemary hadn't been around the past few days.

As soon as she and McGinty arrived, he insisted on seeing to the horses and led them to the small shed that Jack had built in the back. At one time she and Jack had kept two mules, but once they'd settled in the house, they'd decided to keep them at the livery in town. And then, after Jack's death, Rosemary had been forced to sell them to make ends meet.

She entered the home and dropped the saddle bags. Before shedding her duster, she grabbed a bucket and went back outside to the pump for water. Once that task was complete, she hung her coat on a hook by the door, stoked a fire in the stove so that she might heat food for McGinty, and then washed her hands. A pounding at the door startled her.

Thinking it was McGinty, she grabbed a dish towel, dried her fingers, and said, "Come on in!"

She startled when Mortimer Crane stood at the entrance, his wide girth filling the doorway. With a contemplative gaze, he removed his bowler hat.

"Why aren't you in church?" he asked.

Since when did Crane attend services in Wildcat Ridge? After the accident, he'd been spending larger chunks of his time in Cranesville.

"I'm not feeling well," she replied, tucking an errant clump of her blond hair behind an ear.

"Are you avoiding me?"

"No." She straightened her spine, knowing full well she needed to stand her ground. "Should I be?"

He stepped inside. "I couldn't find you at the Assay Office the past few days. I expected you to come to Crane Bank and settle things, but like most of the widows in this town I've got to come looking for you to explain how business works. Let me make this as simple as possible: your lease on the Assay Office won't be renewed, and you're late on the mortgage payment on this place as well."

Despite her lack of money, she wouldn't let him have the satisfaction of turning her out a day early. "That money is due tomorrow."

"Do you have it?"

A flush of humiliation came over her, and she didn't answer.

"I've given you plenty of time, Mrs. Brennan," he continued. "I gave all the widows the entire summer to get their affairs in order. If you're going to accuse me of kicking women out of their homes, then you can stop that train of thought right there. I've been more than generous."

"I had no intention of accusing you of anything." *At least not to your face.*

"I'm not unreasonable, my dear Mrs. Brennan. I'll tell you what. You give me the keys to the Assay Office right now, and I'll let you stay in your home for one more month."

She narrowed her eyes. "And then you'll kick me out of here as well?"

"I'm sure one of the women will take you in. It was very shortsighted of you to have no arrangements pending. I can't help it if you won't make proper plans for your future."

Anger began to replace her shame at being spoken to that way. It was bad enough to lose Jack, but to be treated like nothing more than dirt on the ground was enough to reduce her to tears. But she was determined not to give Crane the satisfaction.

"I think I can clear things up," McGinty said from the doorway.

Crane jumped and spun around. A smile tugged at Rosemary's mouth. Crane was no doubt shocked that his subtle, bullying behavior against the widows had been witnessed.

"Who're you?" Crane demanded.

"The name's Miles McGinty. I'd shake your hand, but I gather you're not a friend of Mrs. Brennan."

Rosemary cleared her throat. "Mr. McGinty, this is Mortimer Crane, the owner of the Gold King Mine."

With the sun behind him and still wearing his hat, McGinty's silhouette made Rosemary think of a dime novel hero.

"The one that blew up?" Miles asked.

"Yes." Rosemary's voice held little cordiality.

Crane tugged on the lapels of his fancy wool coat and tossed a frosty glare over his shoulder at Rosemary before facing McGinty again. "This is a private conversation and of no concern to you."

McGinty crossed his arms and leaned against the doorjamb, effectively boxing Crane in. "Well, now, I think it is my business."

"And how is that?" Crane's tone was dismissive.

"Because I've come to town to pay my respects to my good friend's widow. And I'm also here to become her partner. I'll pay off the money she owes for the Assay Office. And this place, too."

Rosemary froze, shocked by McGinty's pronouncement.

"You can't be serious." Crane's voice boomed off the walls.

McGinty narrowed his eyes. "I'm very serious."

Rosemary's heart pounded. While McGinty's defensive gesture warmed her, he was surely bluffing. She couldn't let him stand in her home and lie, no matter how much she enjoyed watching Crane squirm.

"Mr. McGinty, I thank you for your help, but this isn't necessary," she said quietly.

Her admission seemed to bolster Crane's mood. He turned to her. "I'm tired of playing games. I'll expect you to leave both properties by tomorrow. And so we're clear on this, everything in the Assay Office—the equipment, the reports—it's all mine."

Was Crane concerned that Jack had left something incriminating behind? Rosemary had been in the office for several months now and hadn't found anything out of the ordinary. But maybe she had missed something?

Crane looked back at McGinty. "Because even if you did pay off her debt, I won't let a woman run the

Assay Office any longer. I've been charitable enough letting her pretend to keep her business. Only a man can run it. So, unless you're planning to marry her, we're done here."

A pregnant pause ensued, and Rosemary's heart raced faster with each moment that passed. *No, McGinty. You have no obligation to me.* She wanted to say it aloud, but she refused to give Crane any more ammunition against her.

McGinty gave a nod. "Well, Mr. Crane, you're in luck, because I aim to do just that."

McGinty flicked his gaze to Rosemary, her eyes wide and her cheeks flushed red. She was a woman who bore a second look, and a third, if he was being totally honest, but he could tell that he'd just surprised the life out of her.

He took a deep breath and pushed away from the door, entering the house and facing off against this blustery man that was pushing Rosemary around. Miles hadn't liked it, and he'd quickly crossed a boundary that he shouldn't have with a woman he barely knew, but he couldn't stand by and let her lose everything. He would help her in any way he could. He owed that much to Jack.

Hell, I owe Jack my life. The least I can do is protect his widow.

"I believe we're done here," Miles said. He was taller than Crane, and he stepped close enough to intimidate the man. "I'll meet you at the bank tomorrow. We can settle up then."

Crane took a step back. "This is ridiculous. Anyone can see that this is a sham. I won't allow it."

Rosemary found her voice. "You *did* tell the widows that we had until the end of the summer to settle our debts with you. And you also said that if we had a husband then we could keep our businesses. Plenty of widows witnessed this offer. We could take you before a judge and let him decide."

McGinty pressed forward and Crane finally had had enough. He stepped around Miles and planted his hat atop his head. "I'll see you at the bank at eight o'clock sharp. You haven't settled the debts yet." He gave a scurrilous glance at Rosemary. "This is far from over."

Crane departed, and Miles shut the door.

When he faced Rosemary, she looked as she had

after she'd shot Hector.

"What on earth just happened?" she asked.

"My apologies for my forwardness. I didn't really think it through, except that I wanted to pound some salt into that man."

"You're not the only one." Her voice was barely above a whisper.

She moved to the table, and Miles quickly pulled out a chair so that she could sit. He took a seat opposite her.

She clasped her hands on the yellow tablecloth decorated with tiny blue flowers, looking serene, almost as if she were about to chastise a child. She had nice hands—feminine, with slender fingers.

"First, while I appreciate your offer to help, I can't accept it. Second, you may have just made an enemy of Mortimer Crane, and I hope that it doesn't cause you any trouble. Third—"

He held up his hand. "Please don't concern yourself with my welfare. I've met men like him before. I can handle it. And I hope that you will consider my offer." He paused. "I really would like to help you, Rosemary."

"But … marriage? Please don't take this the wrong way, but I don't want to be married. At least, not again. Not so soon. And you're such a nice-looking man and still young and strong. You will certainly want to be wed one day to a woman who loves you."

Her compliments washed over him, a boon in an otherwise strange conversation. In truth, he'd never thought much about matrimony. He'd never met a woman worth changing his routine for. But Rosemary …

"I owe Jack," he continued. "Let me help you. You can be my wife in name only. I would never ask you to betray your love for Jack."

"But why would you do that? It seems so much to ask of you."

"In the short time I've known you, Rosemary, one thing is clear."

Her expression held a shadow of skepticism.

"You're a stubborn woman."

Her brows lifted, conveying her surprise.

To stave off the likelihood that he'd insulted her, he quickly added, "The fact that you went into the hills alone—I'm guessing you were searching for The Floriana Mine to salvage your situation. Rather than leave this town and your heartache behind, you've chosen to stay. To fight. For your bliss. I have a lot of respect for that. I can see why Jack fell in love with you."

She pressed her lips together, and he thought she might start crying.

"But as strong as you are," he continued, his voice gentle, "it's never easy going it alone. I have nowhere to be, and I have money. Think of it as an investment. We can square up in the future. And I believe we could annul the marriage at some point."

The tears poured forth. "I don't know what to say. It's true that I'm at my wit's end. I have a tiny amount of money, but it's not enough to survive. I have friends, and I could stay with them for a time in town, but that's not a long-term plan. My father …." She wiped her cheeks with her hands. "I can't go to him." She took a deep breath. "I will pay you back for everything. I insist. All right?"

He nodded. "We can draw up an agreement, if you like." He wasn't practicing great business smarts at the moment, but he'd been saving money for several years now with no plan for it. So perhaps this *was* the plan, a fate direct from above.

And as he looked across the table at Rosemary Brennan, widow to Jack—a young man for whom he'd felt a deep responsibility—a sense of purpose and rightness filled him. For the first time in his life, the urge to keep moving abandoned Miles. Maybe he could even let go of his need to find Shady Briggs.

And then there was that twinge in his heart, wanting something it shouldn't. Something that made no sense.

He wanted to stay.

He wanted to help her.

And a small part of him wanted *her*.

Chapter Six

September 1, 1884

Rosemary walked beside McGinty as they headed down Chestnut Street. He had taken a room at the Loftin Boardinghouse, but how long would such an arrangement be needed? If they married, then he would need to live with her. How exactly would that work?

She nodded at the folks they passed and McGinty tipped his hat in a friendly fashion. Rosemary didn't miss the curious glances thrown his way. Her stroll with the man would soon be known throughout Wildcat Ridge. It was difficult to keep a secret around here.

Or maybe it wasn't.

If Jack had doctored reports, how had he hidden it not only from the prospectors but *her*?

She scolded herself for even thinking such a thing about Jack. He would never have been dishonest. It was Alvin whatever-his-last-name-was who was telling bald-faced lies. The degenerate needed a scapegoat and had decided to blame Jack for his own bad fortunes.

Still, if Crane had benefited in some way, then that was an unpleasant coincidence that niggled Rosemary.

They came to Crane Bank and McGinty held the door for her so that she could enter before him. The interior, with its marble floors and two elaborate scrollwork teller cages, had always mesmerized Rosemary with its ornateness. But as much as she admired the building, she had patronized the business as little as possible.

The bank manager approached them, a slender man with graying brown hair. "I'm William Humphries." He shook McGinty's hand. "We've been expecting you."

The manager completely ignored Rosemary, the sting as sharp as if he'd struck her. "Is Mr. Crane here?" she asked, refusing to be dismissed so easily.

Mr. Humphries flicked a glance at her, then gave his attention to McGinty. "No. But I've been instructed to handle everything."

McGinty put a hand at her lower back, making

sure that she wasn't left out of the proceedings.

And so it was that Rosemary's life was handled by two men she hardly knew. Mr. Humphries recorded McGinty's banking information, indicating that it would take a few days of wires and telegrams to finalize the transfer of funds. Papers were signed with the stipulation that more papers would be signed once the monies were received in full.

Never once was Rosemary required to affix her signature. She wanted to laugh outright because it was all so absurd. For a moment, the thought occurred to her that McGinty could be in the very process of swindling her. But she had nothing to take, save her business and her home, both of which she would have lost today if not for McGinty.

They left the bank, and Rosemary felt both relieved and tense. She no longer had Crane breathing down her neck, but now she had a fiancé. A side glance at McGinty left her confused. Once again, relief and tension took up residence in her body. She couldn't explain it, but McGinty represented a safety net she hadn't had since losing Jack. At the same time, his presence tugged at a place in her heart that she had only ever shared with Jack.

Unnerved by her reaction, she walked swiftly to

the Assay Office. Pulling the keys from her reticule, she attempted to unlock the door, but it swung open on its own.

Stunned, she stared at the disarray that greeted her.

McGinty's hand gripped her arm, and he firmly pushed her behind him. "Stay here." He went inside and searched behind the desk and in the back room.

He returned to the main office and stood with his hands on his hips. "Whoever did it is gone." Then he murmured, "I really need to wear my gun at all times."

"Marshal Wentz wouldn't allow it," Rosemary said.

"We'll see about that." His gaze locked with hers. "We need to marry. Immediately."

"Why?"

"So everyone in town—and outside of town—knows that you have a husband who will protect you."

McGinty's rigid stance pulsated with anger.

"What the blazes has happened?" Buster King's voice cut through the maelstrom of emotions swirling in Rosemary's head.

"Oh, Buster." Rosemary spun around and hugged

her friend. "Someone broke in. I have no idea why." But she did. Had Crane sent someone to steal reports? Crane would hardly dirty his own hands. Or could it have been the likes of Alvin or Hector? If more prospectors had been swindled—or believed that they were—it could have been anyone.

But Rosemary knew that the book Jack had used, detailing the assay reports he had produced, wasn't stolen. She had moved it to her house several weeks ago to study in the evenings. It would take time to determine if the thief, or thieves, had taken anything else.

"Well, if they're trying to steal money, there's not much hope of that," Buster said.

The remark made Rosemary laugh, because Buster had known how poor she had become, how many of the women had been down to their last dime. Buster had tried to help where she could, and the horse sale she'd organized two months ago had gotten many of the widows through the summer.

"Madge is at the livery," Rosemary said. "I can go and fetch her for you, but I must apologize. I lost her for a bit while I was in the hills." She quickly added, "However, I found her the next day, and I don't think she suffered any harm. I'm so sorry I didn't look out for her better. But I wanted you to know, in case you think I didn't care for her."

Buster shook her head, her eyes flashing. "She bit you, didn't she?"

Rosemary didn't want to get the horse into trouble, but she also didn't want to lie. She'd had a handful of that from her papa.

"Yes," she dragged out the word. "She did take a little nip."

"Dagnabit, Thad." She looked at her husband, who had crowded in beside her in the doorway. "I told you we didn't have that sorry habit of hers under control."

"My apologies, Rosemary," Thad said. "We'll pay Doc Spense if you have a lasting injury."

"Oh no, I'm fine," Rosemary cut in. "She's a wonderful horse. I really love her. Oh my goodness, my manners." She stepped back. "This is Miles McGinty. He was a friend of Jack's." She hoped that McGinty would make no mention of their encounter with Hector and Alvin.

Miles shook hands with Buster and Thad. "It's a pleasure to meet you both."

"We heard …" Buster hesitated. "We heard that you and Mr. McGinty are to be married."

The rumor mill didn't disappoint. She and McGinty had left the bank less than an hour ago, but already word of Crane and McGinty's agreement had spread. Time to deal with the aftermath. Rosemary nodded. "Yes, that's true."

"That's wonderful," Buster beamed.

"Will you walk with me to the livery?" Rosemary blurted out. "We can both check on Madge together."

Buster seemed to understand the unspoken plea in Rosemary's eyes. She turned to her husband. "Thad, why don't you stay and help Mr. McGinty clean up?"

"I'd appreciate it. And please, call me Miles."

Thad nodded. "Take your time," he said to his wife. "This place is a mess."

Rosemary stepped out of the office, and as soon as she and Buster started walking toward the livery, she locked arms with her so that they could speak as privately as possible.

"I'm a little overwhelmed, Buster."

"About what?"

"McGinty wanting to marry me. I have to tell you that it's just for convenience. He feels responsible on Jack's behalf, and he didn't like Crane pushing me around."

"Well, I like McGinty already. Maybe convenience is just what you need. You're going to have to move past Jack at some point."

Rosemary let her shoulder slump. "I know. It's just hard. I've known McGinty for three days now. How absurd is that? I'm marrying a man I hardly know."

Buster cast a concerned look her way. "Are you afraid of him? Thad or Braxton would pound him if he ever hurt you."

Rosemary shook her head. "No. I can't say why, but I don't believe he'd ever harm me. He's an honorable sort. He paid off my debts to Crane, and he plans to let me run the Assay Office. And he's told me that he doesn't expect me to be a true wife."

"Then I'd say that maybe Jack is still looking out for you."

They walked past the blacksmith.

"Why do you say that?" Rosemary asked.

"Maybe Jack sent Mr. McGinty to help you. We could certainly use another obstacle when it comes to Mortimer Crane. Maybe your McGinty will prove to be the ultimate thorn in Crane's sorry, snake-leathered hide."

Rosemary laughed again. Buster was trying hard

to behave in a more ladylike fashion since marrying Thad several weeks ago, but sometimes the real girl shined through, and Rosemary was heartily glad.

As they walked into the livery, the owner, Jasper Jones, gave a nod in their direction. In his fifties, he was one of a handful of men who had survived after the mining accident.

"Have you come to see Madge?" he asked.

"We have," Rosemary replied.

"She's a feisty one." He chuckled, revealing the gap between his front teeth. "Stay sharp around her."

They found the stall where Madge stood flicking her tail and munching oats.

"I'd like to give you a wedding gift," Buster said.

"That's not necessary," Rosemary insisted. "Like I said, it's not a real wedding."

Buster held up her hand. "Maybe. Maybe not. But let me gift you a horse. A different one than Madge, though."

Rosemary considered the offer, staring at the animal who had been with her during her wilderness adventure. In that moment, her heart swelled. She wanted Madge.

"Could I keep her?" she nodded toward the horse.

"After all the trouble she gave you, you still want

her? Even Jasper thinks she's a handful, and he can handle most any beast."

Madge finished eating and turned around to visit face-to-face.

"I do." Rosemary reached out and stroked the animal's snout. Madge stepped closer, enjoying the contact. "I think we've got a connection."

Buster looked skeptical. "She's sure to bite again."

"I'll duck next time. I'm willing to make a commitment to her."

Buster raised an eyebrow. "And to McGinty?"

Rosemary gave a contemplative nod. She didn't know what the future would hold, but her life was about to change. She and Madge would need to be strong and resolute.

She could do it.

Chapter Seven

September 2, 1884

It was nearly dusk as Miles waited outside the Blessed Church of the Angels on the north end of town, patches of snow dotting the ground in the shadows. The days were often warm, but the evenings saw a drastic drop in temperature.

A quick wedding had been thrown together with the help of Priscilla Gamble, although her father—the preacher—had been killed in the mine explosion. Thankfully, the pastor from Curdy's Crossing, Elijah Stone, had been in Wildcat Ridge today to pick up meat from the butcher, so he'd agreed to perform the ceremony. It had taken all day to organize, but the nuptials were finally about to begin.

Wearing his best shirt and a jacket he had purchased at Tweedie's Mercantile, Miles ran a hand through his short hair and paced back and forth while he waited for the women—Rosemary was inside with Mrs. Gamble, a serious-looking young woman named Thalia Plunkett, and Cora Drummond.

This was to be a marriage of convenience, but anticipation filled him, as if his life was about to take some momentous change in direction.

Well ... it is.

What was he thinking?

Rosemary had professed no interest in him romantically, and he could hardly blame her. She was still reeling from losing Jack, that much was clear. But he couldn't deny a sliver of hope that maybe that could change.

In the meantime, he would watch out for her, protect her.

He'd never anticipated being married. And nothing about this marriage would be of the normal sort. There would be no wedding night. No honeymoon. Would they even live together? They hadn't discussed it. Her home was small. He could stay in the shed, but he suspected the weather would begin to turn soon, and he wouldn't be able to remain outside.

Should he stay at the boardinghouse?

Braxton Gamble approached. "You look a little nervous, Miles." He grinned, adding, "It's not so bad being married."

Miles gave a nod to Priscilla's husband, having met him this morning. "I'm not sure where Rosemary and I will live."

"I suppose it might be uncomfortable staying in the house where she resided with her first husband."

Braxton misunderstood Miles' meaning, but while Miles was certain that Rosemary had filled Priscilla, Miss Plunkett, and Mrs. Drummond in on the fact that their marriage wasn't real, he decided not to hash it out with Gamble, despite that he liked the man. His wife would probably tell him later.

"I built a new place at the hot springs for Priscilla and me," Braxton continued. "Maybe you could do the same."

"That's a thought. But I'm thinking that maybe I could add on to the house she has. I've got some carpentry skills." It was how he'd made a living since his job as a Deputy Marshal had ended.

"That's a great idea. I'm sure she'll want children."

Miles snapped his gaze to the man. *Children?* He hadn't even thought of that one. Unbidden, a future with sons and daughters—and Rosemary by his side—filled his thoughts.

The imagining was much too easy.

Priscilla peeked out the church entrance, her eyes alight with merriment and a big smile on her face. "We're ready."

Feeling as if she had been in the midst of a funnel cloud, Rosemary walked the short distance from the church to her home with Miles at her side.

My husband.

It was done.

Wearing her Sunday best, she had nurtured a tiny hope during the rushed preparations with Priscilla that Miles would be pleased with her appearance. With a sidelong glance, she noted once again that he cut a very fine figure. She supposed it was a good thing that she found her new husband handsome.

When he had looked at her during the ceremony, she had caught a glimpse of … something. As if he wanted her. Truly wanted her. But then the moment had passed as quickly as it had occurred, and now she was certain she had imagined it.

Still, she tucked the moment away in her heart,

holding his gaze as they had recited their vows before Pastor Stone with Priscilla and Braxton serving as witnesses. Cora and Thalia had rounded out the event.

Priscilla had wanted to celebrate after with dinner at the Crystal Café, but it was getting late, and she and Braxton needed to return to the hot springs. In truth, Rosemary didn't feel up to taking her new marriage public just yet.

Miles had suggested they return to her house, and Rosemary had gratefully agreed. Memories of her life with Jack pressed on her.

Oh, Jack. I'm so sorry. I never meant to marry so soon.

A light flickered in the window as they approached the house.

For one brief and wild moment she thought maybe it was her deceased husband, lighting the way through the darkness.

Do you understand why I did it?

But as they neared, Miles held up a hand to halt her progress. "Wait here."

Someone was in the house. A nervous knot twisted in her belly.

Miles took the two steps up the porch quietly. He

peeked in through the window, and then he seemed to relax and waved her to come forward.

As she came to the porch the front door opened, and Dulcina Magnus stood in the entryway.

"What are you doing here?" Rosemary asked. Dulcina had socialized little when she and her first husband had come to town and opened the Last Chance Saloon, but since she had married again—to Gabriel, a striking man she had known in her youth in New Mexico Territory—she was putting forth more of an effort to befriend the other women in town.

Rosemary had always liked her, with her exotic features and lovely singing voice, and impulsively pulled her into an embrace. The display momentarily flustered Dulcina, but she quickly recovered.

"I heard your wonderful news and volunteered to bring you supper on your wedding night." Dulcina smiled and turned to Miles. "I'm Dulcina Magnus, and this is my husband, Gabriel."

"Pleased to meet you both." Miles exchanged handshakes, and they all stepped inside.

The savory aroma of fried chicken filled the air.

"That smells wonderful," Rosemary said.

"There's potatoes and greens and apple

empanadas. Gabriel reminded me to go light with the seasonings on the chicken. Just a hint of chili powder and cilantro."

"How did you make this on such short notice?" Rosemary asked.

Dulcina laughed. "Priscilla mentioned your impending nuptials this morning while we were both at Tweedie's. There were a few others there as well—Mayor Fugit, Eleanora and Grace. I suggested someone ought to bring you both supper, and Priscilla thought it was a fine idea. I insisted that I wanted to do it, and it was fortunate that Olive had just received a fresh order of fryers this morning. We had it all planned."

Gabriel smiled and placed a hand at Dulcina's waist. "My wife doesn't need much of an excuse to cook. She's a natural in the kitchen." He winked. "And I coaxed her into making me a batch of empanadas as well."

"But after the ceremony Priscilla wanted to go to the Crystal Café, only Braxton told her they couldn't," Rosemary said, still surprised by the machinations of her friends.

"It was all a ruse." Dulcina removed her apron. "The two of you can now have a romantic dinner for two."

A protest hung on Rosemary's lips, but the sly look that Dulcina threw her way told her that the woman knew the true nature of her marriage to Miles. Then why was she pretending that Rosemary should act like a besotted bride?

She'd been as such when she'd married Jack.

How quickly her life had changed. It had almost been a year to the day that she had wed the first time. Was she fated to always be a September bride?

Good grief. How many more marriages would she have?

"Thank you," she said to Dulcina. "It was very thoughtful and much appreciated."

"It's no trouble." Dulcina motioned to her husband. "We'll just be on our way so that you both can be alone."

Miles left with them to tend to his horse and Madge in the shed.

Rosemary went to the stove and took stock of the situation: fried chicken in a large ceramic bowl covered with a towel to keep it warm, biscuits, boiled potatoes, and the golden empanada triangles dusted with white sugar. She practically swooned. A pitcher of water and plates and silverware had already been laid out on the table, along with a pretty wildflower arrangement at the center.

A tap on the door, and then Miles entered.

"You don't have to knock," Rosemary said.

"But it's your home." He shut the door.

"I do believe it's *our* home. I think we should eat before everything gets cold."

Miles washed up and they were soon seated across from each other.

She poured them each water and then held up her glass. "A toast?"

"I guess this is cause to celebrate." He tapped her glass with his. His eyes held a glint of mischief. "Mrs. McGinty."

She gulped her water.

"Is it all right that I called you that?"

She took a deep breath and started serving dinner. "Yes, of course. I ought to start getting used to it."

He accepted the plate of food she handed to him. "Rosemary, we should discuss a few practical details."

She began slicing chicken, but her motions with the fork and knife awkwardly slid off the chicken leg. "Of course."

"For the most part, we need the marriage to look

real, if only to keep Mortimer Crane from causing you any more trouble. So I had a thought. What if I built an extra room on the house?"

She frowned at the difficulty she was having getting any meat into her mouth. "That sounds like a big project."

"I've worked as a carpenter, so I've got experience. I could sleep in the shed until then. I don't think it's too cold out just yet."

She pursed her lips and decided to abandon decorum. She picked up the chicken and started eating with her fingers, hunger overcoming her need to exhibit perfect table manners. The different seasonings that Dulcina had used gave the meat a spicy, rich undertone. Rosemary nearly sighed again from the delicious meal.

Grinning, Miles gave up his silverware as well.

She couldn't help but notice the way it transformed his face from aloof to personable. Miles was a charming man. But she wasn't in any position to consider him that way.

And why not, Rosemary? You're his wife now.

Her stomach did a nervous flip, so she pushed that thought aside.

McGinty's demeanor often left her wondering

what he was thinking. He wasn't a man to outwardly wear his emotions. Jack had been like that, too, at least in the beginning of their courtship. Later, she'd come to learn of her husband's penchant for bawdy jokes. A wave of grief passed through her at losing yet another aspect of her life with him.

Did McGinty have a propensity to laugh?

"You don't have to sleep in the shed," she said. "We can make up a pallet for you down here." She indicated the sitting area below the loft where she and Jack had slept.

"It's no trouble," he said, his eyes reflecting an understanding of their situation. "I don't want you to be uncomfortable in your own home."

"And what about you?" She licked her greasy fingers. McGinty didn't seem too shocked by her dinner manners, and for some reason that pleased her. "You deserve to be comfortable, too."

"Well, hopefully I can get the addition built before the first snow. In the meantime, the shed will do just fine."

She reached for a dishtowel to wipe off her fingers. "I hope that we can be friends," she said honestly.

"I hope so, too." The warmth in his brown-eyed

gaze filled her with a sense of anticipation. It were as if she stood on a precipice, and McGinty was there to catch her if she fell.

And a small part of her was happy for it.

Chapter Eight

September 3, 1884

As Miles removed his hat and stepped into the jail that also served as the town marshal's office, Marshal Wentz stood from her seat behind the desk and pushed her braided black hair behind her.

"We met two days ago at the Assay Office." Miles extended a hand, which she clasped firmly then released.

"I remember. McGinty, isn't it?"

He gave a nod.

"You were a U.S. Deputy Marshal," she added.

"News travels fast."

She watched him with a cool eye. "I do my homework. You also married Rosemary Brennan yesterday."

"I did."

Miles sensed her wariness of him, and she didn't offer him a seat. It was just as well. This wasn't a cordial visit.

"I guess congratulations are in order." But she didn't sound very enthusiastic. "What can I do for you?"

"I wanted to know if you learned anything about who might have broken into the Assay Office."

"I questioned everyone on the street. No one at Wells Fargo or the Wildcat Saloon saw anything. When I took Rosemary's statement, she said it didn't look like anything was taken. But if that changes as she cleans up the place, be sure and let me know. Rest assured that I'm keeping an extra eye on that side of town."

"Have you had any other burglaries in town?"

"We did have a break-in last week in a house near where Rosemary lives, but I don't feel the two are related."

"Maybe. Maybe not."

Marshal Wentz sighed. "We've had a lot of men coming and going in this town, and not always of the most upstanding type. You gonna look out for Rosemary?"

"Yes, ma'am."

The marshal's gaze softened. "Then I'm glad you're here. Truthfully, I'm not sure what the perpetrator might've been looking for. Rosemary has had little business, so she has no cash on hand. I suppose her equipment might be worth something, but none of it was missing."

"Did you know Jack?"

The marshal nodded. "Nice fella. Hard-working. He had a lot of business when the mine was open. Do you think he made an enemy?"

"The thought has crossed my mind. Would Mortimer Crane have a vendetta against him?"

"I suppose anything's possible, but take care throwing around that accusation. You don't want to make an enemy of Crane." She held up a hand to stop his protest. "I'm not favoring the man, so put that suspicion aside. If you like, I'll go and question him."

Miles gave a silent affirmation.

"Jack did quite a bit of testing on Crane's behalf," Marshal Wentz added. "If anything, they had a business agreement."

Miles mulled that over. Maybe Jack had gotten himself into something he shouldn't have.

"Will you let me know if you learn anything?" he asked.

"I will."

Miles settled his Stetson atop his head and stepped out onto the wooden boardwalk. As he headed down Front Street, he ran into Braxton Gamble.

"How's your first day of married life?" Braxton asked, knocking the brim of his hat up.

"Much like the days before it," Miles answered honestly. He'd awoken next to Madge and his horse, Pearl, chewing on oats. Not quite how a married man should greet the morning. But Rosemary had at least made him breakfast, although the ham slices were overcooked and the eggs runny.

Braxton was about to continue on his way when he paused and said, "I don't mean to pry, but Priscilla said something to me last night about you and Rosemary marrying for convenience. Is that true?"

"Maybe. Why?"

Gamble shrugged. "She also told me that Rosemary has been through hell since losing Jack, but since you've come to town there's life in her eyes again. I just thought you should know. In case you're thinking of sticking around."

Miles met Braxton's calculated gaze and understood. He and Priscilla cared about Rosemary. And in a very short time, Miles was beginning to care, too.

"I appreciate the observation." Miles gave a nod

and the barest hint of a smile as they parted ways.

He headed to Tweedie's Mercantile, since as near as he could tell there wasn't a sawmill in town. George Tweedie was more than helpful in taking an order of supplies and lumber for the addition that Miles planned to build onto Rosemary's house. He knew someone in Curdy's Crossing who could help, and in fact he thought he could get it all delivered in a day or two.

With his business completed, he walked the short distance to the Assay Office.

When he stepped inside, Rosemary was on her hands and knees, scrubbing the floor. She looked up and blew a wisp of hair away from her face. It struck him how pretty she was, as if he were looking at her for the first time. To keep from staring, he glanced around the office. Everything was clean and in order.

"You've been hard at work," he said.

She pushed to her feet, and he moved quickly to help her. She leaned toward him, brushing against his chest, and then she quickly stepped back and spun around, her hands at her hips, and scanned the room.

And that's when he knew—Rosemary wasn't immune to him.

He suppressed the urge to reach for her. So much

lay between them, not the least of which was Jack.

He did the only thing he could and put the desire for his new wife aside.

"I think everything is in order," she said. "I'm hoping business will improve now that you're officially the owner." She faced him again, her cheeks exhibiting a rosy glow. "If you would be willing to spend some time here, to assure the locals that you're in charge, I could run the tests for you. Or do you know how to sample ore?"

Her blue eyes held him mesmerized.

"Miles?" she prompted.

"Sorry. No, I don't know how to assay samples, but I'll help in any way I can."

She clasped her hands together and smiled. "Good. I think we should get word out that the Assay Office is under new ownership. The local paper isn't really running at the moment, but I could post a notice at City Hall and Tweedie's Mercantile. And maybe Curdy's Crossing. I'll ask our mayor about it."

"Rosemary, I think you should keep Jack's gun with you."

Her happy countenance, although somewhat forced, became pensive, and Miles was sorry to make her worry. "You're concerned about the break-in?" she asked.

"Aren't you?"

Her hesitation seemed odd to him. "Yes, of course. I didn't say anything before, but Jack always kept a small derringer hidden in the back. Just in case."

Miles narrowed his gaze. "Who do *you* think broke in?"

Her eyes snapped to his, and she patted her hair down, then she planted her hands on her hips and dropped her gaze to the floor, apparently in some sort of struggle as to what to say.

"You know that you can trust me," he said.

Those blue eyes landed on him again, triggering anew the desire he had neither wanted nor expected when he'd come to this town. He was in so much damned trouble.

She cleared her throat. "Those men we encountered in the woods—Hector and Alvin—well, Alvin accused Jack of falsifying assay reports." Her voice had lowered to barely a whisper, as if someone might overhear. But they were alone.

"How does he know?"

"Exactly. How does he know?" She squared her

shoulders. "Jack was an honest man. He would never have deceived people. I think Alvin had a run of bad luck and decided to blame it on Jack."

Miles didn't know what to say, because Jack's past—once revealed—would cast Alvin as the aggrieved victim and Jack as the thug. And the last thing Miles wanted was to distress his new wife.

"You think it was Hector and Alvin who broke in?" Miles asked.

"I do."

"Did you tell the marshal this?"

"No."

"Why? She can't do her job if you're not honest with her."

Rosemary's expression crumbled. "I don't want these accusations against Jack made public." In frustration, she wiped at the tears running down her cheeks. "If Jack did do it, then I can only assume that there was a good reason. Right?" The expectant look she gave him made him want to … what? Lie to her? Give her the moon? Kiss her until her thoughts were as muddled as his?

He took a steadying breath. "I can't speak for Jack. Now that you've cleaned the office, did you find anything missing?"

She shook her head. "No."

"The assay reports are all still here?"

"They were never here. I've got Jack's ledger book at the house. I'd taken it home several weeks ago to study what he'd done, and I forgot to bring it back. I haven't had many tests to run." She added in a rush, "But that will change. I know it. And I plan to test the samples I collected when you found me. I assure you, Miles, there *will* be income soon."

"I have faith in you," he said. "All right. We'll keep Alvin's accusation against Jack to ourselves for now. But if you see Hector or Alvin, you need to let me know."

She released a nervous laugh. "Well, that's easy. They're at the Wildcat Saloon."

"Right now?"

She nodded, giving him a sheepish look of apology. "Right now."

Miles stepped through the batwing doors of the saloon and paused while his eyes adjusted to the low-lit interior. The large room had only two tables with chairs, neither occupied. Some of the wall-paneling had been removed, along with half of the bar counter. Miles had overheard chatter among the townsfolk that Crane was steadily moving businesses to Cranesville, in some cases piece by piece. This saloon was obviously one of his recent targets. The widows of Wildcat Ridge had their work cut out for them if they were to keep this town alive.

Along the wall, a bartender was speaking to two men hunched over their drinks. Although their backs were to Miles, it wasn't difficult to recognize Hector and Alvin.

Miles removed his hat, walked over, and leaned his forearms on the countertop. Alvin glanced at him, then did a double-take.

"What the hell are you doin' here?" Alvin sneered.

"Nice to see you, too," Miles replied. "You're not carrying your usual stink, Alvin, so I'm guessing you came to town for a bath."

"That's none of yer business." Alvin pushed his empty glass across the glossy countertop. "Give me another."

The older barkeep poured at least three fingers of the liquid, then looked at Miles, who gave a nod to be served. When he took a sip, he knew he didn't need to concern himself with returning home to Rosemary soused. The liquor was heavily watered down.

From the other side of Alvin, Hector gave a snort of disgust.

Miles ignored him and said, "I just wanted to stop by and say hello." Although his tone was conversational, he watched the men with a steely gaze. "And to tell the both of you to stay away from Rosemary."

Hector rolled his eyes. "We heard she got married yesterday. These women in town are so desperate, but the men marrying them have got to be even more desperate."

Miles stood straighter. "She married me."

Hector choked on his drink. When he could finally speak, he asked, "Why in God's name would you do that?"

"To quote Alvin, that's *none of your business*. What is my business is the two of you. This is a friendly reminder to stay away from her. Am I clear?"

"You don't have to tell me twice," Alvin muttered, hugging his glass to his lips like a babe to his mama's teat. Then he lowered it and added, "I never wanted anything to do with her anyway. She ran out of the woods and harassed *us*. I'd just as soon never set eyes on her again."

William Humphries entered the saloon. "Hector Diaz?"

"That's me," Hector answered.

"Mr. Crane would like to see you."

In an instant Hector went from cocky bravado to stiff discomfort.

"Why would Crane wanna see *you*?" Alvin asked, narrowing his gaze on the man.

"Mr. Diaz is employed by Mr. Crane," Humphries replied.

"What?" Alvin screamed. "Why would you work for that scalawag?"

"Just calm down, Alvin," Hector whispered.

"What kind of work?" Alvin demanded, his voice rising in pitch like a woman scorned.

"The kind that pays money."

"Mr. Diaz is scouting claims for Mr. Crane," Humphries offered, then said in an annoyed voice. "He's waiting, and so am I."

Hector grabbed his hat, coated with a layer of dust, and left with the bank manager.

"Well, isn't that something," Miles remarked as he pulled a coin from his vest and paid the barkeep. "Looks like you're all alone with your principles, Alvin."

"I dunno know what that means, but I can't believe Hector would work for that claim-stealing rat."

Neither could Miles. Hector was up to something. And while Miles had no love of Crane, if he had to pit the two against each other then Hector was in way over his head. Crane would eat him for dinner and spit the bones in the privy.

"Then I guess you and I finally agree on something," Miles said, settling his hat atop his head.

Alvin gave a disgusted grunt and returned to his drink. "And now I've gotta pay the dadblamed bill."

After returning from the saloon, Miles had appeared distracted, so Rosemary closed the Assay Office and suggested they visit the cemetery. It was the entire reason Miles had come to town in the first place, and Rosemary was sorry it had taken her this long to take him. She owed Jack's memory better than that.

She rode Madge while Miles was on Pearl, and they took the road out of town past her house in a companionable silence. She didn't ask about Hector and Alvin. She didn't think either man would attempt something against her, as she now had a husband and an ex-U.S. Deputy Marshal at that. Perhaps she should spread that bit of gossip around to deter any other hooligans from approaching her.

As the late afternoon sun cast a golden hue on the horizon, beams of light played across the Wildcat Ridge Cemetery. An endless array of simple headstones dotted the somber location. Rosemary guided Madge to the western side where Jack's grave stood, glad that she had donned her duster in the chilly air. Miles followed behind.

Expecting the usual crushing wave of grief to sweep over her, she closed her eyes for a moment and took a deep, cleansing breath. When she looked again, taking in the final resting place of so many of the men of town, a sense of stillness came over her.

Peaceful.

It was the only way to describe it.

She halted Madge and dismounted, holding the

reins as she stepped closer to Jack's burial site. Miles stood beside her and removed his hat.

"There's a lot of graves here," he said quietly.

"More than there should be. Not all the bodies could be located or identified, but Jack was one. He wasn't as deep in the mine as some of the others, or at least that's what the rescuers concluded." She tried not to think on that day when Doc Spense had asked her to confirm Jack's remains.

"I wish I had come to visit sooner," Miles said. "I'm sorry that I got here too late. Godspeed, Jack."

For a time, they remained where they stood, the only sounds the soft nicker of one of the horses or the whistle of a bird.

Strands of blond hair danced before Rosemary's eyes, but she didn't try to contain them.

I miss you, Jack. Nothing has been the same since that cold day in March.

At just that moment, a breeze swelled and flowed past them, carrying a breath of warmth, like a caress.

Jack?

A soft laugh escaped her.

"Are you all right?" Miles asked.

Smiling, she said, "Yes. Sometimes the bounty of His grace gives you just what you need when you need it." She held his brown-eyed gaze and was met first with surprise, then compassion.

He gave a nod. "I believe you're right."

Before she thought better of it, she slipped her hand into his and returned her focus to Jack's grave. Miles held firm, and she leaned against him.

It was a relief to share the burden of her grief. The other widows understood better than anyone, but McGinty was the first man she had dared let close to her heart.

Please forgive me, Jack.

As soon as Rosemary stepped into her house, a hammering on the door had her laughing in exasperation.

"Miles, you don't need to knock." She swung open the door to Hester Fugit, mayor of Wildcat Ridge and Rosemary's neighbor.

"Lawsy, lawsy, is that any way to greet me?"

"My apologies."

Hester held a large basket against her ample bosom.

"What have you gone and done?" Rosemary asked.

"I've got supper for you and your new husband. And before you interrupt me, I know he's in the back with the horses, so I wanted to catch you alone for a moment. But first, can I set this down?"

"Oh my, of course." Rosemary stepped back, and Hester deposited her load onto the table. "You didn't need to bring me food."

Hester removed the dishtowel that covered the hearty aroma emanating from the basket, then paused to look at Rosemary. "You know I love you, dear, and please know that I say this with the utmost kindness, but you're a terrible cook, Rosie."

Rosemary frowned.

Hester held up a hand. "Now, now. Before your hair catches fire, let me ask you this. Have you made supper tonight already?"

"I—" But Rosemary couldn't continue. Truthfully, since losing Jack she never cooked anymore, although she had attempted breakfast this morning. It hadn't been much, but Miles hadn't complained. Usually Cora or one of the other widows invited her for a meal or a snack, and it had been enough to get by. In return, Rosemary had gifted much of the bounty from her garden to her friends.

Hester shook her head, a flash of admonition in her eyes. "I know you took good care of Jack. You've just gotten out of practice these past few months, but you need to keep your new husband happy."

"But—"

"I know. It's a marriage of convenience. I've heard." Hester began pulling dishes from the basket. "This is a stew. And there's cornbread and cobbler for dessert." Once the basket was empty, she looked up again. "Rosemary, I'd do anything for you, so let me give you a piece of advice since your mama isn't here to do it, may her soul rest in peace." Hester was one of the few women Rosemary had confided to about her mama.

"Cordelia told me your new man was a U.S. Deputy Marshal," Hester continued. "She did a bit of inquiry and suffice it to say, he's the good sort. Don't let him get away. He'll be a good husband to you. And you deserve it." Hester gave a tug to her shirtwaist. "And I've seen him about town. He's a handsome fella."

The door opened, startling Rosemary, and Miles paused at the entryway. "I didn't realize we had company," he said.

"Miles, I'd like you to meet Hester Fugit. She's our neighbor and the mayor of Wildcat Ridge."

He removed his hat and stepped inside. "It's a pleasure, ma'am."

Hester shook his hand. "Mr. McGinty, I welcome you to Wildcat Ridge. Rosemary is very dear to us, and all the widows in town couldn't be happier for your nuptials, despite the speed of them, but all is forgiven. We're rebuilding, and men like you will be the key to it."

"Hester has brought us supper," Rosemary added, trying to cover for the hesitation she saw in Miles' eyes.

"It smells delicious," he said. "I look forward to it."

Hester grabbed her now empty basket. "Well, I'll leave you two honeymooners to yourselves then."

"It was nice to meet you, Mayor Fugit," Miles said as Rosemary followed Hester onto the porch, who gave one final wave to Miles. Rosemary closed the door in case Hester started on again about holding tight to McGinty.

The woman gave a quick side-hug to Rosemary. "Don't you worry. A group of us hatched a plan at Tweedie's to bring you supper every night this week.

It was heartwarming that Dulcina wanted to be included and went first. So, your only job is to romance your husband. We'll keep his stomach happy and you'll …" Hester chuckled and laid a palm against Rosemary's heated cheek.

Hester was a whirlwind, and Rosemary didn't have the will to argue with her.

"I'll what?" Rosemary teased, keeping her voice low lest Miles overhear their conversation.

"You cheeky girl," Hester said softly. "I can't tell you how nice it is to see a bit of fire in your eyes. Lawsy, lawsy," she dragged out her signature phrase. "God knows we all need a renewed purpose to our lives." She arched an eyebrow. "Do you have any lingerie?"

Rosemary gasped.

Hester smirked. "Don't do anything I wouldn't …." Her voice faded as she walked back to her place.

Rosemary took a steadying breath, then brushed at her skirt and patted her hair before returning to the house and supper with Miles.

Her husband.

Chapter Nine

September 4, 1884

Miles stepped into the Gentlemen Only Salon. After walking Rosemary to the Assay Office, he'd set out to locate Mortimer Crane. The man wasn't at his bank, but the manager had directed Miles to this establishment with a wink.

Miles didn't much care for the man. What was his name? Humphries? He supposed it was because the man did Crane's bidding. Mortimer Crane likely had many such men in his employ.

"To what do I owe the pleasure, Mr. McGinty?" Crane leaned back in his chair and laced his chubby fingers together, resting them upon his ample belly. The small office was decorated in glossy dark wood and furnishings that would befit a man of the East Coast and not an enterprise of a small town in the frontier of Utah Territory. A garish stuffed bear head hung on the opposite wall and a cursory sweep of the room revealed a collection of evocative paintings of naked women. In the short time Miles had been here, one thing was clear—Rosemary had been correct about Crane owning the town. And while the smug bastard had bestowed many niceties on the establishments and townsfolk of Wildcat Ridge, he also wielded his power with an iron fist.

Miles left his hat on. "I've come to talk about Jack Brennan."

"Yes, I understand that you and he were good friends." Crane contemplated him. "But you were very recently employed as a U.S. Deputy Marshal. I'm curious how that friendship grew."

Not much of a surprise that Crane had done some digging into Miles' past. It only confirmed his suspicion that the man had done the same with Jack. And likely many others in town.

"Did you have Jack filing false assay reports on your behalf?" Miles asked.

"That's a bold accusation," Crane replied, derision dripping from his voice. "Especially since you're no longer a lawman. And what are you now? You're the owner of an assay office that you can only run with the help of your new wife, because I suspect that a deputy marshal has little time to learn the intricacies of sampling ore. Your entire livelihood now rests on the abilities of *a woman*. At least Jack was skilled."

"Rosemary has been running things since Jack died. I have every confidence that she can handle it."

Crane snorted. "You will come to rue that day, but that's your business. And now, I've got my own concerns to deal with, so good day to you."

"Who is Hector Diaz?"

"How the devil should I know?"

"He says he works for you."

"In case you haven't noticed, a lot of men work for me."

"Did he break into the Assay Office two days ago on your behalf?"

Crane huffed in exasperation. "Is that what this is about? I don't care about that damned assay office. I let you renew the lease, didn't I? Why would I burglarize it? And I've already spoken with Marshal Wentz about this. You have no authority to question me."

"You'll have to excuse me. Once a lawman, always a lawman." He held Crane's gaze, letting the threat sink in.

Crane narrowed his eyes. "It sounds more like an

illness. Like the Clap."

Miles raised his eyebrows. "Speaking from experience, Crane?"

Crane's cheeks became a ruddy shade. "Young Jack Brennan thought he could run from his past, but that was very shortsighted of him. His beautiful wife had no idea. It would be a shame to break her heart by telling her of it now. But wait—" Crane snapped his fingers "—is that your plan? Is that how you've won her into your bed? By telling her of her dead husband's checkered past? Well then, I guess I can let everyone in town know what Jack was before he settled in Wildcat Ridge."

Anger filled Miles, and he paused to keep his reaction in check. Four years as a marshal had taught him the benefits of restraint, but that didn't mean it was easy, especially with a prig like Crane. "You do what you need to, but let me make one thing clear— Jack Brennan was a good man. Whatever demons were in his past had been put to rest."

"Had they? A man doesn't change his stripes, not even for a woman."

"I'm sure your wife would concur."

Crane stood, his portly frame vibrating with fury. "You may kindly let yourself out."

Miles turned and left. As he departed the Salon and stepped onto the street, he had no doubt that Crane had known of Jack's past. Had the man leveraged it as a means of gaining Jack's participation in an illegal endeavor?

Several townsfolk slid sidelong glances at him as he walked back to Rosemary's house. While people in town had generally been welcoming to him, there was also a frisson of wariness present. He was beginning to appreciate the depth of the wound this town still carried; it would be a while before it fully healed, if it ever did.

Supper last night with Rosemary had been both awkward and pleasant. They had kept the conversation on easy topics—his childhood, her upbringing, and how she had met Jack.

Jack had been happy with Rosemary. It had been abundantly clear in the two letters that Miles had received after Jack had married her and moved to Wildcat Ridge. Miles was certain that Jack would have done anything to protect that.

Guilt weighed on him. If he had come to Wildcat Ridge sooner, maybe he could have set Jack on a better path. Again. Maybe he wouldn't now be dead.

And Rosemary could have lived a long life with

her husband.

A husband who had lied to her.

Now Miles was married to her.

And I'm lying to her as well.

Rosemary was cleaning up after assaying the samples she'd collected the previous week. Several looked promising. She should get back out to the hills—without getting lost this time—and stake a claim just in case. She might still be able to locate The Floriana Mine. Maybe Miles would go with her.

The door opened, and Rosemary smiled at the arrival. "Cora, what a nice surprise."

"Have you been here all day?" her friend asked.

Rosemary nodded. "Yes. I had several prospectors stop in with samples. I hardly had time to break for the noon meal. Marriage is good for business."

Cora shook her head in exasperation. "It's been you all along doing the assays and yet now that you have a husband—who doesn't even work here—it's suddenly acceptable for these men to bring you business? I will never understand the male mind."

"But do you want to?" Rosemary teased. It had been such a good day of work, and now she was looking forward to going home and having supper with Miles. She was enjoying her time with him and how he made her feel like a woman with something to offer again.

Cora's serious expression suddenly worried Rosemary.

"What's wrong?" Rosemary asked.

Cora fiddled with the edge of her sleeve. "Rosie, I've debated whether to tell you, but gossip is running rampant anyway, so it's better if you hear it from a friend." She cleared her throat. "Miles was seen entering the Gentlemen Only Salon today."

As if a bucket of cold water had been dumped on her, Rosemary didn't move. "Well, I'm sure there's a good explanation," she uttered with little sincerity.

Cora sighed. "You've told me it's a marriage of convenience, so I can appreciate that you're not intimate with him. And you've talked about what a good man he is, but I'm afraid the appearance of him so openly disrespecting your vows only two days after marrying you is … well, it's unconscionable. This can only speak to his character in general. I'm not sure you can trust him. And now, you're completely beholden to him financially. I'm concerned." Cora held up a hand to keep Rosemary from speaking. "I've decided that you should come with me to Salt Lake City when I leave in a few weeks. You can stay with Charles and I. Remaining in this town is a sinking ship for you. I know you've never wanted my help, but this is enough."

As Cora spoke, the initial shock over the news of Miles and his dalliance dissolved as quickly as it had come. "But Crane doesn't have any women working for him at the Salon," Rosemary blurted, buoyed by the thought that Miles hadn't been with another woman. News had spread in hushed whispers that Crane had been pressuring some of the widows in town to work for him as paid paramours in order to settle their debt with him, but so far they had evaded Crane's threats.

"There're rumors that he's got women there again."

Rosemary's heart sank once again. But in the next instant, she was filled with angry resolve. She wouldn't be rendered into a state of helplessness by this turn of events. She had survived losing Jack. She could weather Miles' infidelity. It wasn't as if they had a real marriage anyway.

"Cora, I thank you for your generous offer to go to Salt Lake City, but I'm not a ninny to be walked over. If Miles feels the need to visit the Salon, I certainly have no claim to stop him. I'm still convinced, however, that I can keep this business."

Rosemary grabbed her duster from a hook and pulled it on, then gathered her empty lunch pail and a small reticule she carried with her whenever she walked through town, the derringer now tucked inside. She hoped Marshal Wentz wouldn't arrest her for carrying a concealed weapon, but at this point it made her feel safer.

"It's time for me to return home and get supper ready for my husband."

"You're cooking?" Cora asked in surprise.

Rosemary tried not to roll her eyes. "No. You all seem to think I can't crack an egg or cut a slice of bread."

Cora's silent response spoke volumes.

"Nevertheless," Rosemary continued. "Eleanora has graciously offered to come into town and bring something over. Hester rallied the troops on my behalf."

"He doesn't deserve a home-cooked meal," Cora

grumbled. "You should eat it all in front of him."

Rosemary laughed outright. Despite everything, there was a certain amount of dark humor in the situation.

Cora followed her onto the boardwalk and waited while Rosemary locked up.

"You'd better not let him sleep in the house with you," Cora said, fiddling with the hat pinned atop her coiled hair.

"He's in the shed."

Cora squinted and flattened her lips. "Even that's too good for him."

As they crossed the bridge to Front Street, Rosemary shot Cora a look of surprise. "Remind me never to get on your bad side. Charles must always be on his best behavior."

Cora waved a hand in the air. "Oh, good grief. I'm not that much of a shrew. And no marriage is perfect. Not even a fake one, apparently."

They stopped, since it was here that they parted ways.

"Would you like me to come for supper?" Cora asked.

"While I would be happy to have you for a visit, I fear you're just using me." She grinned to remove the sting of her words, and added, "I know how much you love Eleanora's cooking."

Cora released a heartfelt sigh. "I think I could live forever on her rhubarb cobbler alone, and it's always a delight to visit with her little one, Tessa" Then she snapped back to attention. "Don't let McGinty use you."

"I won't."

"If he's a blowhard about it, then come stay with me tonight."

"I will."

Rosemary gave Cora a quick hug, then began walking down Chestnut to the other side of town and her house. Two thoughts danced in her head, opposite in every way.

She was using McGinty far more than he was using her. He benefited in no discernable way in marrying her, and she had gained everything in return—her home, her business, the ability to remain in Wildcat Ridge. She really couldn't begrudge him the need for companionship.

Why, then, did it hurt so much that he'd gone to Crane for a woman?

Chapter Ten

It was late when Miles returned to Rosemary's house. As soon as he walked in, he knew something was wrong.

Rosemary spun around from the stove and planted her hands on her hips, an apron covering her skirt.

"Oh good, you're home." Her forced tone was too bright. "I was about to clean supper up, but you should eat." She waved him to the table.

"I'm sorry I'm late," he said carefully, the chilly atmosphere closing around him.

He hung his hat and coat on the hooks by the door and went to the wash basin to clean up. Rosemary gave him a wide berth, vacating the space like a spooked cat.

Once he'd dried his hands and face with a towel, he took a seat. Rosemary remained standing.

"Aren't you going to eat?" he asked, a rhetorical

question because there was only one plate of food, but he didn't know what else to say.

"I was hungry and decided to have my supper while it was still hot."

"It looks delicious." He dug in.

Rosemary returned to the stove and checked the banked fire, then set a kettle on to boil. "I'll make some tea," she said.

"I went to Cranesville," he said. "It took longer than I planned. That's why I'm late. Did everything go all right at the assay office today?"

"Yes. Fine." She grabbed a dishtowel and began wiping the work counter near the basin. With her back to him, she added, "So you were in Cranesville all day?"

He sopped up the last of the gravy with a biscuit and savored the bite. Once he'd swallowed, he answered, "For the most part."

She turned to him, her expression no longer congenial, her cheeks splotched with pink. "I feel the need to say something about your behavior today."

"My what?"

"I know you went to the Gentlemen Only Salon. You should know that more than one person saw you." Her chest heaved, and she appeared as if she were having trouble breathing.

"Rosemary—"

"I understand that we don't have a real marriage, but appearances can be everything. And while I'm sure you must feel the need for … companionship … I really must ask that you not do it in broad daylight, or so soon after our marriage has taken place."

He stood.

"Just as a courtesy," she continued. "I'm not telling you *not* to go, I just …"

He moved to stand before her, near enough that he could indulge a subtle inhale of her distinctive smell of soap tinged with roses. "I wasn't with another woman today."

Her eyes flicked upward and met his.

"I went to see Crane."

"Why?"

Her rosy lips distracted him, and thoughts of kissing her took up every empty space in his head.

But Rosemary wasn't like other women he'd been with. She might be his wife, but he was well aware he had no claim to her.

He didn't move. It wasn't lost on him that she remained rooted in place as well.

"Because I think he had something to do with the

break-in at the Assay Office."

"Marshal Wentz cleared him," she replied, her voice carrying a slight tremble. He hoped it was for him.

"Maybe, but I decided to go to Cranesville to talk to the assayer there, a young man by the name of Frankie Edwards. Do you know him?"

She shook her head. "Are you trying to replace me?" Her eyes flashed with amusement.

"No. I wanted to know if Crane had a noose around him as well."

Her gaze dimmed. "You think that Crane was using Jack?"

"It's crossed my mind. And while Frankie didn't say much about his relationship with Crane, he did admit something interesting."

"What's that?"

"He said Jack told him that you're the best assayer in these parts."

Her eyes widened in surprise. "Then why don't I get more business?"

"I'll give you one guess."

Her eyes narrowed. "Crane. Is it because he can't control me?"

"I think it's much simpler than that. You're a

woman."

"Do you agree with him?"

"That you're a woman?" he teased.

She laughed, giving him a playful nudge against his chest. He caught her hand and held it, looking at their clasped fingers as he spoke. "I want you to be who you are, Rosemary, and I would never stand in your way."

He raised his eyes to hers, searching for an answer to his unspoken question. Eyes that reflected a stark longing for him, giving him hope.

"I've only known you for days," she said, her voice barely above a whisper. "I don't understand this connection."

He raised his free hand to her face and lightly ran a finger along her cheek. "I knew the first moment I saw you."

She didn't pull away. "You mean when I was running from Hector?"

"I wasn't thinking clearly." His thumb skimmed along her lower lip. "I jumped off my horse and blew any advantage I had. My only thought was to stop him. It's a good thing you saved me."

She closed her eyes and swayed toward him. He took the opening and bent his head to capture her mouth with his.

For a long moment, he held the kiss, keeping his hunger for her in check. The feel of her in his arms and the taste of her lips was enough to both soothe his need and ignite it. She yielded, pressing into him, and he allowed himself a moment of indulgence. He gave the kind of kiss a husband bestowed on his wife, one that promised a long night spent together.

But he was no fool.

He broke the contact and rested his forehead against hers, his breathing heavy.

"I'd be happy to see this marriage be a real one," he said. "But I know it's too soon." He raised his head and looked into her bright blue eyes, her face flushed, her lips swollen.

She nodded. "If we …"

He released her and stepped back but grabbed her hand once again.

"If I share your bed, we'll be well and truly married," he said. "I want you to be certain."

"What about you? You've been a bachelor all these years, and now you're saddled with a wife. You might not want to stay either."

She was wrong. He had no idea how he had fallen for her so quickly, but he had. Jack had described her in his letters, triggering a sense of familiarity in Miles even then. When he'd learned of Jack's death, why had he traveled all this way to pay his respects? Had it truly been for Jack? Or had he wanted to meet Rosemary? She had written him one letter after he had inquired about a visit. He still had that letter. It meant something to him that he'd never understood or been able to explain.

"I'm staying, Rosemary. I'll only leave if you ask me to."

"What are you saying? That this is my choice?"

"Yes."

The kettle whistled. Miles moved past her and removed it from the stovetop. "I'll make a fire and we'll have some tea," he said. "And then we'll go to bed." He glanced over his shoulder. She watched him with uncertainty in her eyes. "Separately." But he couldn't help but add, "Mrs. McGinty."

Chapter Eleven

September 5, 1884

After an amiable breakfast with his wife that consisted of sticky porridge—he was coming to realize that Rosemary wasn't terribly blessed with cooking skills—he had walked her to the Assay Office.

After the kiss last night, he had kept his hands to himself. He didn't want to push too fast too soon. They had time. Truly, they had all the time in the world. He could wait for her.

Miles stopped at the mercantile and Mr. Tweedie informed him that the lumber he had ordered was being delivered to Rosemary's house as they spoke. Miles headed there and was soon immersed in planning and organizing the new addition. He would add it on the far side of the sitting room that sat below the loft. He could build most of it before cutting a door, to minimize the cool of the nights seeping into the house.

Around midday, Cordelia Wentz appeared.

He set a stack of lumber on the pile off to the side and tipped his hat. "Marshal. What can I do for you?"

She crossed her arms and sighed. "Well, for starters, you can stop doing my job."

He pulled off the work gloves and sat on one of the porch steps. "I apologize if I've overstepped. I just—"

She held up a hand. "I know. You're ready to throw Crane in jail." She glanced around, but there was little activity at Miner's Row across the street. With the Gold King Mine no longer open, the workers had moved on to Cranesville. Still, with word of Braxton Gamble's Arrastra Mine hiring, men were slowly returning.

Marshal Wentz stepped closer and said, "It's complicated. But I can't have you questioning him. I already took care of it. He has an alibi."

Miles scoffed. "You don't really think he would commit the break-in himself, do you?"

"McGinty, watch your tone."

He gave a curt nod. He wasn't normally so hot-headed, and Cordelia was fully in her rights to be annoyed with his meddling. He would have felt the same if he were in her position.

"He's filed a complaint against you," Cordelia said.

"Can't fight his own battles, can he?"

"Well, be that as it may, I'm here to give you a friendly warning. Back off. I'm keeping my eye on the Assay Office, and I'm generally aware of the chatter in town amongst the prospectors and the like. My guess is that it was an out-of-towner looking for cash. I don't think there will be a repeat."

Miles considered telling her about his suspicions about Crane and the scam he had been running with Jack's help, but Rosemary didn't want Jack's name dragged through the mud. And neither did Miles. And unfortunately he didn't have any proof, just a gut feeling, and he could well imagine the cluck of disapproval from Marshal Wentz over that fact.

An ugly thought reared and before he thought better, he said it aloud. "Marshal Wentz, just how close are you to Crane?"

She went rigid and her eyes flashed with anger. That told him all he needed to know. He held up both hands in defeat.

"My apologies," he said. "I had to ask. Crane controls so many people already."

"He doesn't control me." Cordelia's voice held a steely edge.

"I'll do whatever I can to protect Rosemary."

Cordelia's stance relaxed a bit. "I know. And we're all happy that she has you in her corner, real marriage or not." She cast him a hooded gaze. "It's clear to anyone and their uncle that you have feelings for the girl."

So much for keeping his cards close to the vest.

"If you know something about Crane," Cordelia said, "something that includes *clear evidence*, then I'm all ears, McGinty."

"I understand."

"All right then. I'll leave you to your work." She walked away, then turned back. "If things pick up in town like we're hoping, then I might need a new deputy. I had Braxton Gamble for a bit, but he's got his hands full with the hot springs and his new mine. You interested?"

"I'm gonna take a pass on that. I've got plenty to keep me busy these days."

She nodded and glanced at the piles of lumber. "You building something?"

"An extra room." *For me.*

"Smart man. A babe will come before you know

it. Have a good day, McGinty." The marshal departed.

A babe.

He glanced at the space that would soon be a bedroom. He had thought Rosemary would take the room, leaving the loft for Miles, sparing him from freezing through the winter.

But maybe that would change.

He hoped so.

Rosemary was finishing up testing the samples she had found from when she had encountered Hector and Alvin. The first time she had met Miles.

Her heart kicked up a notch just thinking about him. And that kiss.

It would be so easy to give in to her attraction to him—they were married, there was nothing to stop it. Except the voice of reason pounding in her head.

She had been impulsive when she had married Jack, and she didn't want to think that she would simply rush into another marriage so blithely.

And she had been happy with Jack, devoted to

him. So what did it mean that she could develop feelings for someone else so soon after losing Jack?

Guilt pressed on her.

As easy as McGinty was on the eyes, as much as she enjoyed talking with him, and as much as she wanted to lean on him during times when she felt low—she needed to be smarter than that.

She needed to keep him out of her bed. At least for now.

The door opened to the office and Hector entered.

Rosemary immediately grabbed her reticule and retrieved her derringer, pointing it at the man.

"Easy, easy. I'm not gonna hurt you." He wobbled as he walked toward her.

"Why are you limping?" she demanded. "I didn't shoot you before."

"You sure in tarnation did!" he rebutted in a whiny voice.

She scowled at him. "You need to leave. My husband won't be happy that you're here."

He chuckled. "How could I forget? Everyone in town is talking about your new husband. Many prospectors secretly think you run better tests than anyone else in these parts. What a load of hogwash."

"I'm not going to stand here while you insult me.

Were you the one that broke in here a few days ago?"

He eyed her with an assessing stare. "I heard about that, but nope, it wasn't me. What was taken?"

"That's none of your business."

His forward motion was finally halted by the counter, but Rosemary hadn't lowered the gun.

"I've got a proposition for you," he said.

Rosemary prepared to shoot him.

He gave her a look of disgust. "No! Nothing like that. You're too skinny for me anyway. I've got a business proposition. I've heard the talk around town, how you widows hate Mortimer Crane."

"We don't hate him." Not exactly the truth, but it would never bode well to rile Crane's temper, and they sure didn't need someone like Hector stirring the pot for them.

"What if I said that I had proof that your husband—*your first one*—" he added with a smirk "—was falsifying assay reports to help Crane gain valuable claims."

"And what proof would this be?" She debated how she could escape the company of this vile man. She'd never get past him to the front door, and if she turned and ran out the back door to where her assayer's oven was located, he'd probably follow and get her before she screamed for help.

"Well, now, if I told you that, we'd have no way to make a deal. I need something from you."

"Let me guess," she said with a dawning realization, "you need assay reports. The reports that Jack kept here." She spoke as if she were addressing a six-year-old child. "But they're not here, are they?" she said with mock surprise. "You already knew that, though, because you ransacked this place and couldn't find them."

He flashed her a look of disgust. "All right, Miss Smartypants. You think you've got it all figured out, but if we work together, we can nail Crane. And he'll pay up mighty fine for it in order to stay out of jail. And I'll split it with you."

Rosemary was so stunned, she could hardly get the next words out. "You want me to help you blackmail Mortimer Crane? You must be drinking that mine run-off water, because you're addled something fierce."

"Wouldn't you like to have something to hold over Crane? Imagine the leverage it would give you in town. You could run your business in peace, and you could help the other women. They'd all praise you as a saint."

Outrage filled her. This man sauntered in and expected her to break the law, just like that.

But Crane is a criminal.

She wasn't the only one who had struggled against him. Many of the women in town had been on the receiving end of his threatening and bullying behavior that often crossed a moral and legal line.

He believed himself to be above the law.

Oh, to watch him squirm. The image brought her too much pleasure.

But must she lower herself to Crane's level to fight him?

There was an even bigger issue, however. If Hector truly did have evidence of Jack's deception, then her husband—her *first* husband, as Hector had pointed out—wasn't the man she had thought he was.

Jack had duped her. What else had he withheld? Had their entire marriage been a sham?

I can't believe you would have done this, Jack. You knew how I felt about the lies my papa told. You knew how important honesty was to me.

The man she had married had been intense and hard-working, doting on her as if the sun had risen and set at her feet. She had returned that love with almost a flush of desperation since she had never met anyone like him.

The more she was forced to look, however, the bigger the cracks in her marriage to Jack widened, aided and abetted by her own blind faith in him.

Her father hadn't wanted her to marry him. Had that been the deciding factor in why she *had*?

Hector's lips spread into a malicious grin. "I can see that I've peaked your interest."

Rosemary lowered the derringer, her arms aching from holding it for so long. "I'm not agreeing to anything. But how would you prove this?"

"I need the report book that Jack kept."

She knew it. He'd broken into the office. "You're a thief!"

"I am not. I never actually *took* the book."

"Now you're just splitting hairs."

"Do you want in or not?" he demanded.

"How would you prove Jack's duplicity?"

Hector paused, throwing a glance at the front door to make sure no one was about to enter. "There's a second book," he said quietly.

Rosemary frowned. "A second book of what?"

"Your beloved Jack kept a separate book of assay reports, meant only for Crane."

"And you know this because …"

"I've seen it."

"How do you know it's not the *actual* book of reports?"

He leaned closer. "Because you have a book, too, don't you?"

She did. And it seemed in order. She'd read through it several times in the past few months. It made sense now. Hector needed her book as a comparison. Only by putting the two ledgers side-by-side could any discrepancies be confirmed.

"What exactly do you propose?" she asked, feeling sullied just asking, but she needed to see what he had. She needed to know if it was in Jack's handwriting.

"Show me yours and I'll show you mine." He wiggled his eyebrows.

She didn't hide her expression of disgust.

"Meet me outside of town tonight at the bend in the Black Bear River. And come alone."

Rosemary leveled a cool gaze at the miscreant. She would go, of course, if only to put this business about Jack to rest. But as for going alone, she was no fool.

Oh, Hector. I have no intention of doing that.

Chapter Twelve

That evening, Miles entered the house to an aroma that had his stomach rumbling. While working outside on the addition, he'd seen Mrs. Loftin arrive from the boardinghouse with a large basket, and he suspected that they were once again the recipients of a charity supper.

He organized his work space as quickly as he could, and then he headed inside while the food was still warm.

Rosemary was setting the table, so he washed up and took a seat.

"It smells delicious," he remarked.

He hadn't kissed her again and a tension hung in the air, but alongside it was a warm feeling of home and hearth.

Rosemary sat and placed a napkin on her lap. Roasted pork and boiled potatoes beckoned. "We have Mrs. Loftin to thank for this meal," she said.

He poured a glass of water for her and then himself. "You have a really supportive group of friends."

She nodded, buttering her biscuit. "There's something you should know."

He gave her his full attention.

"I'm not really a very good cook. Unfortunately, these mouth-watering meals won't last much longer."

He laughed at her confession. It hadn't taken long to conclude that cooking wasn't her forte.

"I just wanted to be honest with you," she added.

The comment brought him up short, and once again the weight of deceiving her about Jack's past pressed on him.

"I promise I'll try harder," she added in a rush. "I wasn't raised by my mama. I thought she was dead, but it turned out that she wasn't. Anyway, it's a long story."

"Do you see her now?" he asked.

"No. She's since passed away. Growing up, my papa spent more time teaching me about rocks than household skills, although I did spend time with my aunt. Jack always said he loved my dirt soup."

He frowned. *Dirt soup?*

"It's a jest," she said, raising an eyebrow.

He should tell her the truth. "Rosemary—"

"And I have something else to tell you," she interrupted. "Hector came to see me today claiming to have evidence of Jack's illegal wrongdoings at the Assay Office, and I agreed to meet him later by the river."

He stilled. "You did what?"

"Before you lecture me about safety and such, please note that I'm telling you about it. Hector told me to come alone, but of course I'm not a dolt. I wouldn't do that. I want you to accompany me."

Anger and worry halted his words, and he stared at Rosemary's beautiful face. She had loved Jack, of that he had no doubt. And Miles had loved Jack, too, like a brother, like the one he had lost. But pain sliced through him. She took these ridiculous chances because of Jack. Would she ever feel this way about him?

She shifted in her seat, then scratched her head below her bun, jiggling a few blond strands free. Would she let it down if he asked?

"You're not going off into the woods by yourself," he said with a tone that surprised even him.

"No, I'm not," she replied. "You're going to come with me."

"For someone claiming not to be a dolt, you're sure acting like one."

She straightened. "I am not."

This was getting out of hand. "Then it's time we told Marshal Wentz about all of this and let her handle it."

Her eyes widened, reminding him of a cornered animal. "But then word will get out, and the gossip will be too much. Everyone will talk about what Jack did. What if it's not true? Hector claims to have a different report book that Jack kept, one that he prepared specifically for Crane. He wants me to bring my book. If we can compare them, then I'm certain I can disprove this ridiculous notion that Jack was behaving like a criminal."

Ah, hell. Miles clenched his jaw. "There's something you should know," he said.

"Don't say it." She shot to her feet. "Don't tell me that Jack probably *did* do it. You were his friend, but I was *his wife*. I think I knew him better than that. And I'm going to see Hector tonight with or without your help."

She took her plate to the counter and started

stacking the dirty dishes in the sink.

Miles' chair scraped on the floor as he left the table and came to stand behind her. "I'm sorry. I didn't mean to fight with you. Let me meet Hector. Let me deal with whatever he thinks he might have."

She ceased organizing the bowls and plates and didn't move.

"I feel it's my duty to protect you now," he continued, tucking a stray hair behind her ear, unable to keep his hands from her.

A visible shiver rippled through her.

She hung her head. "This is very complicated, Miles."

Her words encompassed more than the issue with Hector and the report books. She was talking about the two of them.

"I know." He rested his hand at the nape of her neck. "If I let you go, then you must do something for me."

She spun around. "No!"

Startled, he took a step back. "I didn't tell you what it was yet."

"I ... I don't want you to leave me." She took a steadying breath. "I'm still grieving Jack, and it's left me confused. Not the grieving, but *you*. I'm utterly confounded by your presence. I know that I'm probably not the best wife around, but I don't want you to go." She raised her eyes to his. "I want to make this work."

Her sudden outburst filled him with hope. He watched her with amusement as he sought to clear up her misunderstanding. "I meant if I let you go meet Hector."

"Oh."

"But I'm glad that you want to make this work." He leaned close. "I'm probably not the best husband around either."

"Don't underestimate yourself, McGinty."

He smiled and kissed her, a simple peck. She grinned, so he kissed her again. Soon she was engulfed in his embrace, her arms wrapped around his neck, and she matched McGinty's growing passion with her own. When he finally released her, he couldn't help but be pleased by the bewildered look on her face. With clarity, his own selfish motives surfaced. He didn't want to halt the progress he was making with her, and so he let pass the opportunity to tell her about Jack and his very criminal past. He was a cad, and he knew it.

Not feeling too pleased with himself, he guided

her to the table. "Will you please eat your supper? Then we'll go find Hector, but you'll stay hidden while I talk to him."

"All right."

Rosemary stood near a copse of trees by the Black Bear River while Miles went looking for Hector. With no moonlight, Rosemary strained to see into the darkness, the tip of her nose cold from the crisp night air, the gurgle of the river beyond whispering to her.

She held the reins of Madge and Pearl, and luckily they were calm and quiet. Worry gnawed at her over Miles. They had agreed that she would keep the report book with her and that Miles would instead take a gun with him to talk to Hector. If he decided it was safe, only then would he allow Rosemary into the discussion.

Her body still hummed from McGinty's kiss, making her feel as if she had awoken from a deep and lonely sleep. Living without Jack had been unbearable some days, but since meeting Miles, she was slowly coming back to life.

His touch awakened every feminine part of her, and she couldn't help but wonder what it would be like to truly be his wife. But what if it was a mistake? What if she brought him into her bed only to realize later that they couldn't get along? At least if she remained chaste, she could end the marriage in the eyes of God, her conscience mostly clear as long as the Maker could forgive a few impure thoughts of McGinty. And if she didn't remain untouched, then what did that mean regarding her life with Jack? The only man she had ever been with was Jack. It was wrong of her to want another so soon after her husband's death.

Wasn't it?

Miles materialized from the shadows.

The grim look on his face jolted her. "What's wrong?" she asked.

"Hector's dead."

"What?"

He reached for her horse. "I'm taking you back home."

"But shouldn't we do something?"

"I'll return and deal with this, and then I'm telling Marshal Wentz."

The worrisome feeling started bothering her again. When Miles indicated for her to mount Madge, she stopped and said, "Can I see him?"

"Who? Hector?"

"Yes."

"Rosemary, you don't need to view this."

What about the book he claimed to have?

She didn't voice the thought aloud, however, knowing how selfish it would sound. She reasoned that even Hector deserved a prayer after such a grim ending, despite the dubious state of the man's character. "Please," she said.

Miles didn't move. In the darkness she couldn't see his face well, but she knew he was conflicted about whether to grant her request.

He finally gave a nod and secured the horses, then he pulled his gun and clasped her hand as he led her to Hector's body.

Unsettled by what she would see, she braced for the worst. His body lay on its side atop a bed of pine needles, a metallic smell accosting her. *Blood.*

"How?" she whispered.

"Gunshot."

They halted about five feet away. She closed her eyes and recited a prayer for Hector's soul to receive absolution for his sins, of which there were no doubt many.

"What about the book?" she asked, her voice barely above a whisper.

"It's not here."

Hector's body moved, and Rosemary screamed. McGinty pushed her behind him and raised his pistol.

Peeking around McGinty's shoulder, her voice was frantic as she said, "He's alive."

Chapter Thirteen

Miles remained at the shed door while Doc Spense and Cora Drummond tended to Hector's gunshot wound, Rosemary hovering nearby. He would have been happy to leave the man where he lay by the river, but Rosemary had insisted they couldn't abandon him there to die. They had staunched the blood flowing from the shoulder wound as best they could, and then Miles had put the unconscious man across his horse and brought him back to Rosemary's house. Since there was no way in hell he was about to let the man inside, the shed was the only option.

Actually, that wasn't true. Miles had wanted to take Hector to Doc Spense's office, leave him there, and then head straight to Marshal Wentz so that she could deal with the aftermath of whatever criminal activity that Hector was currently embroiled in. But Rosemary had insisted they keep this quiet.

He knew why. She wanted that second book, but there had been no sign of it. She was still determined to protect Jack, so it was up to Miles to protect her. And he would do just that. At first light, he would return to the river to search for clues.

Doc Spense gathered his medical equipment, tucked everything into his bag, and stepped away from Hector and the two women.

"What's the verdict, Doc?" Miles asked, keeping his voice low.

"He's alive for now. I removed the bullet, and if he makes it through the next few days then he should survive." He glanced around the interior of the shed, the two horses off to the side. "This isn't the best place for a patient to recover."

"It's complicated," Miles said, echoing Rosemary's words from earlier.

The doctor nodded. "So I gathered. We really should tell Cordelia."

"I understand, but I'm asking for a bit of time first."

"For what?"

"The less you know, the better, but I'm concerned about Rosemary's safety."

"The only reason to stay quiet about something

in this town is because the trail could lead back to Crane. Would that be true?"

"You didn't hear it from me."

The doctor sighed. "I certainly don't want to be an accessory to harboring a fugitive."

"Hector's not a fugitive, but it might be for the best if no one knows he's alive. For now."

The doctor's grunt of response carried both agreement and caution. "I'll come back tomorrow to check on him. Try to give him broth and don't let him use the shoulder. Rosemary said she's got laudanum on hand, so use that for pain."

"Got it." Miles held out his hand. "Thank you."

The doctor shook it. "Are you plannin' on stickin' around?"

"Yes, sir. I am."

"I'm glad to hear it."

The doctor left.

Just before dawn, Rosemary rose from her bed, pulled on a robe over her sleeping gown, and made her way to the kitchen to stoke the fire and prepare coffee for Miles. He soon quietly entered the house.

"How is Hector?" she asked.

"Still alive." Miles went to the sink and washed up.

"I've laundered your clothes." She nodded to a neatly stacked pile atop a chair. "You can change here. You don't need to go back to the shed."

He had remained near Hector's unconscious body throughout the night, and she could see the fatigue lining his face.

He gave a nod and stepped away from the kitchen to change his shirt.

Rosemary turned to speak again but stopped when she was greeted by Miles' naked upper body, faced away from her. He was tall, lean, and well-muscled. For a moment, she simply watched, mesmerized.

It was an odd reaction. She had certainly seen Jack unclothed many times, but her heart and mind responded as if McGinty were some new and never-before-seen specimen. But it was the tug in her belly—an awakening of her body's cravings—that drained the air from her lungs.

She missed the intimacy she had shared with Jack. She missed what it was like to lie with a man, to have him hold her, to join with him in a way that was private and precious.

She wanted Miles in this way.

He pulled a clean shirt over his head and faced her, his movements ceasing as soon as his eyes met hers with a flicker of surprise.

"You don't need to go back to the shed at all anymore," she added, her breathing shallow, her heart pounding.

He stopped securing the buttons and his arms fell to his sides. "Are you certain?"

She stepped forward until they were only inches apart. "Yes."

She took his hand and led him to the loft ladder. As sunrise bathed the land with the soft light of a new day, Rosemary gave her body to McGinty.

But more than that, she gave him her heart.

Chapter Fourteen

September 9, 1884

Miles stood at the doorway of the shed and crossed his arms. After three days, Hector had finally awoken, and despite being weak from a gunshot wound and lack of food, he was as ornery as a cornered bear just up from hibernation.

"You stole it!" Hector pointed a finger toward Miles, but his reclined position upon a pile of hay gave him little advantage in this standoff.

Miles shook his head and sighed.

"Stop moving around," Doc Spense groused from beside the man.

Miles had summoned the doctor as soon as Hector had opened his beady little eyes.

Someone poked him, and he turned to see Rosemary standing just outside the shed. The sight of his wife brought a smile to his face. Although caring for Hector had been a thorn he could have done without, the past few days had been filled with more happiness than he had ever anticipated.

He would have swooped his wife into a more than friendly embrace, but they had an audience. He gave a nod to Mrs. Drummond, who stood behind Rosemary.

His joy soon fled when he noticed Alvin.

"Don't worry," Rosemary said in a rush, clasping his arm. "He just wants to see Hector."

Miles leaned close to her and said in a low voice, "If you keep bringing people here, Hector's presence won't remain much of a secret."

"I know."

Miles stepped aside, and everyone crowded inside.

"I'm not sure I wanna know why you're lying injured in this woman's shed." Alvin gave a nod toward Rosemary.

Miles placed himself in front of his wife. He certainly didn't trust this cretin.

"But I've got some news," Alvin added, "and I've been lookin' everywhere for you."

"What are you talking about?" Hector demanded.

"Our samples came back good. I forgive you for workin' for Crane, but now you can stop. I filed a claim. For the both of us. You've gotta get up off your arse and help me work it."

Hector narrowed his eyes and shifted his gaze to Rosemary. "Did *she* do the assay?"

"Nah. It was that Frankie in Cranesville who dun it." Alvin frowned. "Although for some reason, he wanted me to go to Mrs. Brennan."

"It's Mrs. McGinty now," Miles cut in, never taking his eyes off Alvin.

The man scrunched his face and rolled his eyes.

"Why is Frankie sending me business?" Rosemary asked.

Alvin huffed. "Beats me. I'm certainly never coming to you with my samples. Are you holdin' Hector prisoner?"

"I'd like to know what in tarnation is going on in here," Marshal Wentz's voice interrupted, startling everyone.

As Miles sat on the porch, he explained everything to the marshal. Rosemary and Mrs. Drummond were inside the house—Miles wasn't going to leave them alone with Alvin, who had remained in the shed with the doctor and Hector.

"So Jack Brennan was running a scam," Cordelia said. "Why would he do that?"

While Miles had revealed his and Rosemary's scuffle with the two prospectors, the accusations the two men had leveled against Jack, and the supposed existence of a second book of assay reports, he hadn't mentioned Jack's criminal past or the fact that Mortimer Crane had known about it.

"I think he did it on Crane's behalf," Miles said, stepping around the truth.

"For money?"

"What else?"

Cordelia looked at him expectantly. "Then where is this money? Because Rosemary suffered as much as any of the widows when we lost our men in the mine accident. I doubt she was sitting on a pile of cash the whole time."

"I'm guessing Jack kept it hidden from her."

"Or Jack didn't do it for money. *If* what you're saying is true, then it makes far more sense that Crane had something to hold over Brennan." She gave Miles a contemplative look. "Would you know something about that, too?"

Wentz was smarter than he had given her credit.

When he didn't answer, she muttered under her breath, "Jack had a past. A past he kept from his wife."

Miles gave a silent affirmation, since Rosemary was only a few feet away inside the house.

"Where's the book?" Cordelia asked.

"I don't know. I searched the area near Hector's shooting, and all I found were a few footprints."

"Who shot Hector?"

"He doesn't know. He said he never saw the man, or men, who did it."

She stood. "I'll talk to this Cranesville assayer, Frankie, and I'll talk to Crane again, but I'm guessing you know how that will go. We need the second book. You do know that I need to take Rosemary's assay book, right? We can't have it floating around. I'll lock it up in the safe at the jail."

He opened the front door. Rosemary sat at the kitchen table drinking coffee with Cora.

"Cordelia wants Jack's assay book," he said.

"No."

He stepped further into the house and Wentz entered behind him.

"Rosemary, I just want to keep it safe," Cordelia

said. "It could be an important piece of evidence, especially if we can locate this supposed second book."

"I understand, but I'm not relinquishing the book."

Her sharp tone surprised Miles.

"This is out of our hands now," he said to his wife. "It's time to let Marshal Wentz take over."

Thankfully, Cordelia hadn't threatened him with obstruction of justice. He no longer wore the badge, and his interference had most certainly impeded her own investigation.

"The book belongs to me," Rosemary said. "It's in a safe place. And if you locate the second book, that also belongs to me since it was Jack's, or purported to be. If you find it, I'll expect it returned to me."

The determined set of her jaw brooked no argument.

"All right," Marshal Wentz said, backing off. "I'll be on my way. Will Hector be staying with you then?"

Rosemary jerked her chin up and down. "I was just trying to do the right thing by helping him."

Cordelia frowned. "I hope you know what you're

doing." She glanced at Miles. "But you've got McGinty, and he seems to have your back." And then she added more directly to Miles, "I'll leave it to you to keep me informed of any changes."

Miles didn't miss the resignation in the marshal's gaze. He could swear she was giving him her blessing to help in the ongoing investigation.

As she left the house, she muttered again. "As if you'd listen anyway if I told you to stop acting like a lawman."

A knock at the door revealed Eleanora's sister, Grace, on the other side. Rosemary was heartily grateful to see a friendly face. And Grace was bearing food.

"You all are spoiling me," Rosemary said, stepping back for the taller woman to enter.

"I'm happy to help." Grace deposited supper on the table.

"I'll return your dishes to you first thing tomorrow."

Grace waved her off. "There's no hurry." She

directed her dark gaze at Rosemary. "Is everything all right?"

"Of course. Why wouldn't it be?"

"Well, you have a man in your shed who's been shot."

She should have known bringing Alvin here would be a mistake. But the prospector had been so worried. When he'd come to see her, she simply couldn't lie about his friend's whereabouts, no matter how much Alvin disliked her. Not only had he led Cordelia here, but now the entire town likely knew about Hector Diaz and his whereabouts. Rosemary hoped that wouldn't be a problem.

"He's not well, and I was trying to be a good Samaritan."

"Do you think the men who shot him will come here?"

Yes, that thought hadn't escaped Rosemary, but she didn't want to worry her friend. "No. We've talked with Cordelia. And Miles was a U.S. Marshal." Rosemary smiled brightly, knowing her argument was weak. "I'll be fine. Thank you so much for supper. I hope to repay the kindness one day."

"No, no. Please don't feel obliged. Hester told us that you needed to focus on your marriage, so it was no trouble to make a little extra for supper and share it with you both."

"I can cook, Grace."

"Of course, you can." Grace scooted around the table and gave Rosemary a conciliatory hug.

"Oh, all right." Rosemary's shoulders sagged. "I can't cook. I know that. But if you ever need an assay done, I'll do it for free. Deal?"

Grace smiled. "Deal." Then in her most pragmatic countenance, she added, "Now, please get that prospector out of your shed."

Rosemary nodded. "I will. Probably tomorrow. One more night of rest and he should be well enough to leave."

She hoped.

As Grace departed, Miles entered the house and they sat for supper. Thankfully, he didn't press her further regarding the whereabouts of Jack's assay book.

Chapter Fifteen

September 10, 1884

Rosemary organized her assay instruments—a tray of cupels, an iron mortar and pestle, sieves to sift the pulverized mixtures, and her scales for weight measurements—then wiped off the work space with a rag as the office door opened.

"We're about to close," she said, not looking up.

"This won't take long."

Her gaze snapped to Mortimer Crane's presence filling the confined office space. A man stood behind him whom Rosemary didn't recognize. Probably Crane's bodyguard. She'd heard rumors that he had men who protected him, but she thought it odd he had one with him while visiting her. Did Crane expect her to turn violent?

Rosemary wiped her hands on her apron. "What can I do for you, Mr. Crane?"

"I wanted to stop in and see how your business

was faring."

"Just fine, thank you." She flicked her eyes to the bodyguard hovering near Crane, his gaze unyielding. She didn't much care for the guns he openly wore.

Crane removed his bowler hat and set it on the counter. "I understand you've been getting more assays."

Rosemary gave a curt nod. "Some."

"That's good. I'd hate to see you get behind on the lease, but my understanding was that your new husband was going to be running things."

"He's in charge, but I'm doing much of the day-to-day work."

"I see. I suppose the inner workings of the assay field are complex. I understand that you're acquainted with a man named Hector Diaz. I was vexed to hear that you've taken him into your home, as I understand he was recently involved in a shooting, which sounds dreadful. Do you really think you should be associating with such a piece of scum?"

"He's not in my home. I let him sleep in my shed." Crane was up to something. "Would you know why he was shot?" she blurted, her heart pounding.

"Good Lord. Of course not. Rosemary dear, are you accusing me of something?"

She didn't answer, the bodyguard's presence looming large.

"All right, I'll get to the point." He reached inside his jacket and withdrew some papers. He unfolded the top one and gave a heavy sigh. "I really didn't want to burden you with this information, but I truly feel that I must help you. I could never live with myself if something were to happen to you."

Rosemary narrowed her eyes. Crane only ever helped himself.

He pushed a faded Wanted poster toward her.

Dread filled her.

No, no, no.

Feeling sick in the pit of her stomach, she stared at the likeness of three men.

Wanted for three train robberies in the Oklahoma Territory. Everett "Shady" Briggs. Gordy "Snake" Newcomb. Johnny "Bawdy" Briggs.

"I fear the last man is the spitting image of your Jack."

Crane's voice became muted as Rosemary's world shifted. She had done her best to hold to the love that she and Jack had shared, to honor it as if it were a precious jewel, something pure in a world that was anything but. She had convinced herself that Hector and his talk of a second book was merely a ruse, especially after he'd been mysteriously shot and the book in question had never surfaced.

She even secretly had wondered if Hector hadn't shot himself. It had been yet another reason she had wanted to keep him close. It gave her the perfect opportunity to catch him in his lies.

But Hector hadn't deceived her.

It had been Jack.

Johnny.

She gripped the edge of the counter, distantly aware that she didn't want to show any weakness in front of Crane, but tears filled her eyes anyway, blurring the image of the man her husband had been.

"I can see that you didn't know," Crane said, his voice sickly sweet and grating on her nerves. "And honestly, I wouldn't ever have told you if I hadn't thought it necessary. Jack—Johnny—is gone, and I could see no reason to smear the memories you had of him. But then I learned of Johnny's connection to your *new* husband."

Crane unfolded a newspaper article and laid it atop the Wanted poster. He clucked under his breath.

"It was shocking, really. Miles McGinty had been a prisoner of Johnny's gang. They even tortured him. He managed to escape, although it doesn't say how in this news piece, but how odd that he maintained a friendship with Johnny Briggs. And now he's married to *you*. I'm concerned for you, Rosemary. I feel you may be in the middle of something."

Her thoughts were swirling. Miles knew that Jack was Johnny? Why hadn't he told her?

"What do you mean?" she asked.

Crane leaned forward as if he was about to share a juicy secret with her. "Revenge," he whispered. "I'm thinking that McGinty never forgave those men for what they did to him. He's probably been hunting each of them down one by one."

The pain that Crane's words unleashed filled her with anger. "You're suggesting that he married me as a vendetta?"

"I can't say. I'm merely the messenger, but I can help you. This talk of a second assay book is damning evidence against Jack, and I don't want to put you through any more nastiness. Give the book to me, and I'll take care of it."

"You'll take care of what?"

He gave a flick of his head toward the man

behind him. "I can have McGinty taken care of. You can keep your business and your home. I can protect you, Rosemary."

Horrified by what Crane was implying, she kept her reaction in check. Maybe McGinty had used her, but the last thing she wanted was for him to be killed.

"You really want that book, don't you?" she asked.

Crane's friendly demeanor was replaced with an icy glare. "If you help me, I'll help you. It's as simple as that. Otherwise, I can't protect you. I would advise you to bring that book to my salon by tomorrow. If you cross me, you'll find yourself working there. Mark my words."

He snapped his hat off the counter and put it on his head. Without another word, he and his bodyguard left.

As if Crane had punched the very air from her, she struggled to breathe as she stared at the papers he had left behind.

Jack hadn't just doctored a few assay reports, he had held people at gun point and robbed not just one train, but many. Had he killed anyone? She felt ill at the thought. What of the money that he'd possessed when they had come to Wildcat Ridge? He had told her he had worked for it, had saved, had wanted to make a good life for her. But had it been stolen?

And Miles had known all of it. He'd been one of several U.S. marshals following Jack's gang. And he'd been taken prisoner by them.

Tortured.

What did that do to a man?

Miles seemed to be decent and honest, but she'd been wrong about Jack, so chances were she was wrong about her new husband, too.

Miles had hardly known her and yet he'd wanted to marry her. Too quickly.

He obviously wanted something from her. But what?

It didn't really matter.

She knew what she had to do.

Chapter Sixteen

Rosemary was late coming home, so Miles unpacked the dinner that had been delivered earlier by a widow named Garnet Chandler. He had managed to get rid of Hector, or at least Hector had assured him he would be gone from the shed by this evening. The man had mentioned that Alvin was going to help him to the boardinghouse, which was fine by Miles. They were at a standoff over that damned second book. Rosemary had never revealed where she had hidden the first one, so maybe it was just as well that neither one would ever be seen again.

Miles finished setting the food on the table, then glanced out the window. It was almost dark, and worry crept in. The front door opened just as he was reaching for his coat.

"I was coming to look for you," he said.

Rosemary's cheeks were bright pink, and her eyes flashed like an angry wildcat.

Something was wrong. "What is it?" he asked.

She shut the door. "I think we need to talk." She opened her reticule and dropped two papers onto the table.

His stomach took a tumble.

She knows.

There was no doubt in his mind.

She spun around. "I can see by the look on your face that you know what those are."

"Rosemary—"

"For once, could *someone* tell me the truth?" she demanded.

"I'll tell you everything."

Her chin came up. "Now you will? Why not before? Did you think so little of me? Or better yet, am I just a means to an end?"

He released a pent-up breath, blasted by a sudden bout of nerves.

He'd had her, and now he was going to lose her.

Regret knifed through him.

He should have told her sooner.

Suppressing the urge to take her in his arms, he stepped around her and scanned the Wanted poster and the newspaper article she'd placed on the table. For one wild moment, he'd hoped that maybe the evidence in her possession wasn't what he thought it was. Maybe he could still fix this.

Maybe …

The least he could do now was tell her the truth. He pulled out a chair from the table and sat, indicating for her to do the same. "Have a seat."

Their supper was getting cold, but he'd lost his appetite.

She didn't oblige him. Instead, she went to the sink and leaned against it, still wearing her duster, her arms crossed, her demeanor telling him in no uncertain terms that he wasn't welcome anywhere near her.

"Jack's real name was Johnny Briggs," he said. "I don't know much about his childhood, but by the time he was twelve years old, he'd been running petty crimes and rode with a gang led by his brother, a man named Everett, but most people referred to him as Shady Briggs.

"I told you about how my brother had been killed. It was Shady Briggs who did it. When I became a U.S. Deputy Marshal, I had only one goal in mind— to find him and bring him to justice." He took a deep breath. "It took a while, but eventually I was able to infiltrate the gang, and I was accepted. I was close to bringing them all in when one of the other deputies blew my cover and Shady took me hostage. He had me for more than a week, and like the ruthless man that he was, he didn't kill me right away but instead sought to make me suffer." Memories of that time were incomplete, and Miles had consciously made an effort not to dwell on them. "Johnny took pity on me—we'd become close while I was with them—and he eventually helped me to escape. Obviously, he couldn't stay with Shady after that. His life was now in as much jeopardy as mine, so I helped him start over with a new name and a new life."

"Didn't he have to go to jail for his crimes?"

Miles paused. No one knew this part of the story, because he had let a criminal go and Johnny had needed to disappear. "I helped him get away. I told officials that Johnny had died during my escape."

"Why would you do that? Why would you risk your career for him?"

"Johnny wasn't a bad sort. I'd grown fond of him, and I wanted to help. In many ways, he became the brother I had lost. It wasn't logical, I'll agree, but when he begged me to let him go … well, I let him. After he created a new identity, we stayed in contact. That probably wasn't wise either, but I worried over him. When he met you, it changed his life. He wanted a fresh start. He wanted to do good."

"Then why did he doctor those reports?"

"I don't know exactly why, but my guess is that Crane somehow learned of Jack's past life as Johnny and was blackmailing him over it."

"But if Crane knew, then others must know, too." Concern crept into her voice.

He nodded. "That thought has crossed my mind."

"Is that why you came here?"

"I came here because I'd lost yet another *brother* and I was heartbroken. And I came here for you."

"But you're still looking for this Shady Briggs?"

He paused. Although he had stopped actively searching for the man, he couldn't deny that if given the chance, he'd go after the son-of-a-bitch. "I am," he answered honestly.

"And you think he'll come here."

"A possibility."

"So, you marrying me was just a ruse?" she asked.

No. *Maybe.* "A little," he reluctantly admitted. There was a certain bittersweet relief in coming clean.

"Am I some kind of bait for this man?"

"I know you may not believe me, but I love you, Rosemary. I think I've loved you since before I ever came to Wildcat Ridge. Jack's letters about you— and your letter to me after he died—they … I don't know how to describe it, but they got to me."

"If Jack hadn't died, then you were planning to come here and steal me from him?"

"No! Of course not. I loved Johnny, too." He raked a hand through his hair. "I didn't plan to love you, but I do. And I can't take it back now. And I'm not sorry I married you."

"How can I believe you? How can I believe anything you have to say? Jack lied to me. You lied to me. And all this business between you and Jack and Shady Briggs means nothing to me.

"I abhor lying. When I was a child, I had no recollection of my mama. Papa told me she had died, and for many years he fed that lie while I mourned losing her before I'd ever had a chance to know her. Then, one day when I was fourteen, a woman showed up and claimed to be her. Turned out, she hadn't died, but she'd had a life of hardship from an opium addiction. When she had gotten herself to a better place, she wanted a relationship with me—had wanted one for years before that—but my papa had denied her. By the time she found me I only had a very short time with her because she was very sick and passed away not long after. I've never forgiven my father for keeping her from me."

"Rosemary—"

"So you see," she continued as if he hadn't spoken, "I'm well accustomed to moving on after a betrayal."

"What are you saying?"

"I'm saying that we're done. I want you out."

Panic filled him. "I don't want to lose you."

With tears in her eyes, she whispered, "You never really had me."

Chapter Seventeen

September 11, 1884

Miles sat at the dining table at Loftin's Boardinghouse staring into his cup of coffee. The other boarders had all eaten their breakfast and departed, but Miles had nowhere to go. The life he had quickly built with Rosemary was over. He needed to convince her that their marriage could work, because during the short time he had known her he had come to need her as he'd never needed anyone, not Billy, not Jack.

How could he not?

She was a connection he had never sought and yet fit so perfectly into his life that he couldn't imagine his days without her.

She was right to be angry. He couldn't fault her for that. But perhaps if he gave her a few days to accept what he'd told her, then maybe he could stop over and suggest they talk.

The plan filled him with hope. He started to eat the eggs, bacon, and fried potatoes that Mrs. Loftin had left for him, cold from his time spent dwelling over the ruination of his life.

He may have lost his brother and Johnny, but he'd be damned if he lost Rosemary, too.

"There you are."

Marshal Wentz stood across the room, holding her hat. Her grim expression was the one constant he'd come to expect from her.

"What have I done now?" he asked.

She tilted her head. "I'm guessing you've done plenty since you're here and not at home with your wife. Did she throw you out already?"

He surprised himself by laughing. "You sound like you're about to tell me, *I told you so*."

"Nah." She sighed. "I hope you'll make amends because I think you both might actually love each other."

His heartbeat ricocheted in his chest. Did he dare hope that Rosemary could feel anything close to love for him?

"But I've been looking for you," she continued. "I've caught wind of something I think you ought to know. Mortimer Crane has brought a man to town who seems very interested in *you*."

"Who?"

"He's calling himself Houseman, but one of Crane's men was overheard using a different name. Shady Briggs."

His pulse pounded. "He's here?"

"Everett 'Shady' Briggs is wanted for murder in the Oklahoma Territory, along with train robbery." The sharp edge of her voice was enough to slice a man. "It's my job to arrest such a criminal if he surfaces in my jurisdiction."

Miles watched and waited, sensing that she wasn't finished.

She scoffed. "Oh hell, McGinty. I can tell there's business here, and I'm guessing it runs deep. If you want my help, I'll give it." She paused, then gave a derisive nod. "But I can see that you don't."

"This isn't your concern, Cordelia," he said softly. "I won't risk your life."

Or Rosemary's. It was why he was here. While he had certainly felt compelled to protect her from Mortimer Crane, somewhere in the back of his mind he had always thought Shady might come looking for Johnny, bringing him right to Rosemary's doorstep.

"All right then," she said. "I deputize you, but

this is no job offer. It'll give you the right to do what you need when you confront the man. Then it's back to your carpentry."

He gave a nod and stood. "I need to see Rosemary."

"I'm afraid you just missed her."

"What do you mean?"

"She was seen riding out-of-town at daybreak."

"To where?"

"Toward Braxton's mine."

It was where Miles had found her the first time he'd met her. Why was she going back? There could only be one reason. She was still searching for The Floriana Mine and the hope of a bonanza that would make her flush with capital. And then she would divorce him.

Rosemary was more careful this time, both with plotting her course once she rode beyond Braxton's Arrastra Mine and taking extra care with Madge so that the horse wouldn't take a nibble out of an important body part.

Using the survey tools her father had given her, she meticulously charted her journey into a small notebook, silently berating herself for not doing so the first time. She had overestimated her abilities, assuming she would be able to make her way in the wilderness because she had done it before with Jack—no, Johnny. A growl grew in her chest.

Had Jack even loved her? Had their entire marriage been a lie?

He'd been vague about his childhood, but said he'd been on his own since he was a lad, and she hadn't pressed him any further, imagining that it was simply a painful subject for him.

When they'd met, she'd liked the energy he exuded, as if he held the world in the palm of his hands. It had drawn her quickly to him and she'd fallen head-over-heels in love, wanting to be with him so much that she had rebelled against her papa's wishes to take more time to consider marriage.

So she had run off with Jack, blinded by her infatuation with him.

And what of Miles?

While Jack had been exuberant and headstrong, Miles was almost the opposite—quiet and steadfast—but her passion for him ran just as deep.

Falling face-first into love seemed to be her strong suit.

Tears flowed and the previously repressed scream she released startled Madge, causing the horse to snap her teeth into the air. The gesture shocked Rosemary's crying into submission.

"Alright, Madge." She patted the animal's neck. "I'll stop feeling sorry for myself."

Feisty indeed.

She had supplies to last for three days, and the weather appeared to be holding. She was determined to find that mine.

By mid-afternoon, she came to a mountain with scree fields emptying to a common point at the base on its north side. This matched a description that Jack had jotted down in his notebook. She was certain she hadn't been here before—she had really gotten turned around when she'd lost Madge a few weeks ago—so she decided this bore a second look.

Having skirted a small lake, she dismounted at the edge of the tree line and tethered Madge's reins near a dense patch of grass. "Don't go anywhere. Just stay here and bite the grass."

She double-checked that the horse was secure, then took her gun, a canteen of water, an empty burlap sack to hold samples, a shovel, and a flame lamp, and headed out. The golden leaves of the aspen trees fluttered in the breeze, and beyond were black-reddish cliffs rising high.

Scanning the area, a notch in the rock caught her eye. She began to climb.

While Braxton had managed to find one of the old Spanish mines, Rosemary knew the odds of finding another were low. And even if found, the Spaniards, having utilized Indian slaves, had likely worked as much gold as they could, leaving little behind. There were also tales of Mexicans later working mines in this area, returning south to their homeland with pack burros heavily laden with their spoils, further depleting the deposits.

It was difficult to extract gold in this area, so it was usually a byproduct of silver or copper. Still, the rumors of a cache of riches had long persisted. The Mormons had befriended the Ute Indians and that relationship had yielded the location of several mines.

It would be a longshot, Rosemary knew, for her to find anything remotely viable. Despite that every man in her life—her papa, Jack, Miles—had failed her, she refused to fall into despair. If all of this had taught her anything, it was that her life was in her own hands.

The climb became steeper and Rosemary perspired beneath her clothing despite the chill in the air. As she crested a ledge, she stopped.

A symbol of a cross was etched on the rock. Excitement coursed through her.

There were plenty of crosses found in these parts along trails and carved into trees. Jack had told her these were to mark the Spanish Trail, originating in Mexico and going north.

But why would such an etching be on a cliffside?

To mark the location of a mine.

She climbed higher, searching for a tunnel opening. She was soon rewarded with an entrance hidden in a slight alcove. She lit her lamp and carefully made her way into the belly of the mountain.

Chapter Eighteen

It hadn't been difficult to track Rosemary, although there had been more than one set of hoof prints. Was there someone with her? Marshal Wentz hadn't mentioned a companion. With unease dogging his every move, Miles continuously scanned his surroundings.

He lost the trail twice—once through a muddy area and then near a small lake—but after intense searching, he soon had it again. He spied Madge tied off in the distance, grazing, but no sign of his wife.

Something didn't feel right. He cut to the west so that he could remain in a dense cluster of pine trees. Once he was hidden, he secured Pearl and pulled a spyglass from his gear. It was definitely Madge grazing across the lake.

The cliff standing vigil at the water's edge was no doubt an irresistible draw to prospectors everywhere. Thoughts of Rosemary crawling through an abandoned mine tunnel chilled him, and he decided to find her before she hurt herself trying to find gold in some far-fetched dream.

Movement beyond caught his eye, and he halted.

In disbelief, he checked his viewfinder.

It was Alvin, riding a burro. And beside him, atop a fine-looking sorrel Quarter horse, wearing a fancy wool duster and his ever-present bowler hat, was Mortimer Crane.

Rosemary stepped gingerly as she moved deeper into the belly of the mountain. The air was stale, and the only light came from her lamp. Scratching and scurrying noises sounded from either side, and she had to grit her teeth to keep moving.

The tunnel had wooden shoring and appeared to have been blasted out in parts. Farther in, dirt walls were crumbling to the ground, and broken timber littered the path.

She paused and took a steadying breath. Her actions were foolhardy to say the least, and she began to second-guess herself.

So far, she had seen nothing to indicate any type of mineral deposits, let alone gold. Clearly whoever had mined this claim—and she had to guess it was decades if not centuries old—had already cleared the most promising veins.

Braxton was in the process of hiring men to work his mine, and while his samples—which she had run herself—were promising, there was no guarantee what he would find in the end.

She stopped abruptly at a slithering sound just beyond the glow of the light.

I need to get out of here.

She turned and ran into a shoring that partially blocked the path. The wood split with a crack. Rosemary screamed and fell to her hands and knees, falling dirt knocking the lamp from her hands. She tucked her face toward her chest as dust filled the air, holding her breath so she didn't inhale the musty particles.

Coughing, she sat up and strained to see what had happened. The lamp, lying on its side about three feet away, cast a weak glimmer and her eyes settled on the wall that had just partially given way. Luckily, she wasn't trapped. Pushing her feet, she was determined to get out of here.

In the settling dust, a big burlap sack became visible. She moved closer and eyed it up and down. With her nerves on edge, her imagination was running a little wild, so she gave the bag a good kick in case it was filled with snakes, but her boot hit something hard.

She carefully took hold of the top of the material and tried to lift the bag, straining her arm muscles until her neck hurt. It was much too heavy to lift.

She pulled a knife from her boot—she had decided to be better armed this time out—and struggled to cut a hole in the material. When she was finally able to reach inside, her fingers touched something solid and cool against her skin.

With some idea what it might be, she twisted one of the bars free and held it in the palm of her hand. She hurried over to the lamp to confirm her suspicions.

Her heart stampeded in her chest, and her excited exhalations filled the eerie silence.

It was a gold bullion.

Miles remained concealed, waiting to see what Crane and Alvin were up to. As they skirted along the lake's edge toward Madge, two additional riders appeared. He recognized Hector immediately, but it was the second man who had him swearing under his breath.

Shady Briggs.

Rage coursed through him.

I could take him out right now with one sniper shot.

The loss of Billy was as sharp and deep as the day his brother had died. How Miles had remained in the gang as long as he had without killing Shady in his sleep, he'll never know.

The man didn't deserve to live.

Rosemary.

The whisper cut through the maelstrom swirling in his head.

Was Billy speaking to him from beyond? Or maybe it was Johnny, back from the dead.

Miles sought to calm the wild turn of his thoughts. He had Rosemary to consider. He couldn't fight for her or try to win her back from a jail cell. She deserved better, especially after the pain of Johnny's lies.

He lifted his scope to watch the men. Hector and Shady joined Crane and Alvin, and all of them began to converse. They appeared to be getting along, which gave Miles pause. Were they all in cahoots together? Then, Alvin pointed at Madge.

Miles didn't have to guess that they all knew Rosemary was nearby.

Miles readied to gather his horse and move to a closer vantage point when yet another rider appeared. It was Frankie Edwards, the young assayer from Cranesville.

Why is he here?

Rosemary was obviously searching this mountainside and would soon return, walking right into this posse of men, none having her best interests at heart. Except maybe Frankie, but Miles wouldn't put much stock in it.

Miles had to get to her before these men did.

Chapter Nineteen

As Rosemary left the cliffside and entered the trees, movement caught her eye. She slipped the one bar of bullion she'd taken from the bag in the tunnel into her coat pocket and readied her gun. Several men were gathered together. She hunkered down to hide, sensing danger.

Had she been followed, or was this gathering of questionable males merely a coincidence?

She recognized Hector and Alvin, but two of the men she didn't know.

And the fifth one … what the devil? It was Mortimer Crane.

Why is he here?

He preferred plush furnishings, fine whiskey, and an ample bosom if the rumors floating around about his unfaithfulness to his marriage were true. Riding for miles into the wilderness would hardly be on his agenda. Were the two men she didn't recognize more bodyguards?

Was Crane running some kind of thug meeting?

Or worse, was he here to kill Hector?

She had little affection for Diaz, but after letting him live in her shed for several days she'd acquired a desire to see him remain alive. And he had apparently been in possession of a book that would prove very incriminating to Crane. It was likely that Crane had arranged for Hector to be shot the first time.

With dismay, she realized that all of them had already seen Madge. Her horse stood nearby, her ears pricked back in irritation. The arrival of the men and their mounts had clearly disquieted the animal.

Thankfully, none of the new arrivals appeared interested in hurting or harassing her horse. And her horse was still here, unlike a few weeks ago when Rosemary had been lost in this very wilderness, forced to approach the likes of Hector and Alvin.

She certainly couldn't expose herself this time. She held no illusions that they would treat her well.

The group of men conversed for a time, which she couldn't hear, and then the taller, unknown man began to search the ground, moving toward her.

Oh good Lord.

He was tracking her.

Moving quickly, she scrambled to her left and crouched low behind a bush, praying that he wouldn't see her.

Just as swiftly, the faultiness in that thinking blared in her head.

Your footprints, Rosemary!

There was no way she could lose the man.

Impulsively, she stood and raised her gun. "Hold it right there," she said.

The man stopped and raised his hands slightly, narrowing his gaze as he looked her up and down. He bore a striking resemblance to Jack.

He grinned. "You must be the lovely Rosemary I've heard so much about."

The others crowded around the man.

Crane stepped behind Hector when his eyes landed on her gun. "Mrs. Brennan put that down," he demanded with a sputter of unease.

She gripped the weapon in both hands, holding her position with false confidence, but she wasn't about to let any of them know that.

"What are you doing here?" she asked.

"I could ask the same of you," Crane said. "I can't believe your new husband allows you to run traipsing through the wilderness like this. It's disgraceful. And now you're handling a gun like a common ruffian."

Ignoring Crane, she waved her gun toward the tall man. "Who are you?"

"My name is Everett. I knew your husband." He chuckled. "Or should I say husbands."

His hands lowered a bit and she waved the gun back and forth, encompassing all of them. "Every one of you keep your hands up."

They all complied.

Everett continued to speak. "I understand you married Johnny. He was my little brother, but I'm guessing you didn't know that as you tried to set him on the path to redemption, which was very admirable, I suppose." A flash of pain crossed his roughened features. "I was sorry to hear he died in that mining accident. You probably won't believe me, but he was kin and I favored him the most."

"You must be Shady Briggs," Rosemary said.

"You *have* heard of me. Excellent." His amused expression went hard again. "But I have to say that I must question your motives in marrying Johnny, especially since you married Miles McGinty so soon after Johnny's death. But, of course, I didn't know

McGinty by that name when he worked with me. He called himself Ben Wheeler back then. We had a bit of a falling out, but I'm guessing you don't know too much about that either. It's really a shame how much your husbands have lied to you."

"What is it that you want exactly, Mr. Briggs?" Rosemary asked.

"Just two things, really." His voice took on a steely edge. "I want the money Johnny stole from me."

When he paused, Rosemary shook her head. "I don't have it."

"That I don't believe, but I'm willing to forgo it for the second thing."

"What's that?"

"Ben Wheeler's head on a spike."

Rosemary's hands trembled, and she gripped the gun tighter to hold it steady.

"Wait a minute," Crane cut in. "I never said you could murder the man."

Briggs cast a cool glance in Crane's direction. "I never asked your permission."

Crane shifted from leg to leg, looking uncomfortable. "But this will all get tied to me. I will not be an accomplice to this. If you kill McGinty, you must do it far from here. Do you understand me? You owe me that much for giving you the information about his whereabouts in the first place."

Rosemary didn't know how to proceed. She could hardly corral all five men and leave without any trouble. And if they found the bullion in her pocket, they would surely want to know where she had found it.

"So, you've followed me," she blurted out. She pointed the gun at Hector. "Why are you here?"

"Briggs made me come. I saw you leave early this morning. Is it because you fought with McGinty last night?"

"So McGinty's not here?" Briggs demanded.

Hector ignored him. "Besides," he continued, glaring at Rosemary, "you've got the second book."

That again! "No," she answered. "I don't."

"Then where the hell is it? I've gone over and over it in my mind, and you're the only one who would've taken it. And you shot me too, didn't you?"

"I did not."

"You're holding a gun right now," he cried. "And you'd already shot me once before anyway."

"Rosemary." Crane's cheeks had taken on a scarlet hue. "You need to give me that second book."

"Don't give it to him," Hector cut in. "He's a thief, and that book will prove it."

"Now, Hector," Alvin said. "Maybe we should just give Crane the ledgers and such."

"Why would you say that?" Hector asked.

"Crane here is gonna give us a decent claim. All we gotta do is give him that book."

"I don't have it," Rosemary answered, trying to figure out how to get to Madge and escape back to town. She was beginning to feel a little better that they wouldn't find the old mine she'd just found. Instead, it would seem they'd all come her to find her. Or, in Shady Briggs' case, Miles.

She really needed to tell Marshal Wentz about all of this.

Briggs sighed. "Can we stay on subject here? I don't give a flying fig about some book."

"I have it." The shorter man that Rosemary didn't recognize had spoken.

"What did you say?" Crane shifted and pushed into the man, who stumbled back but quickly righted himself.

"*Who* is this?" Rosemary asked.

The man held a hand up to keep Crane back. "You stand down, sir." He glanced toward

Rosemary. "I'm Frankie Edwards. I'm the assayer in Cranesville."

"Who works for me, I might add," Crane ground out. "If you have the book, Edwards, then you better damned well give it to me right now."

"No sir, I'm not gonna do that." Frankie looked at her again. "Can I come over there?"

Praying she wasn't making a mistake, she gave a curt nod. Frankie Edwards came to stand beside her and the protection of her gun.

"That book is mine!" Hector demanded.

Frankie shifted nervously. "No, it's not. Mrs. Brennan, er … Mrs. McGinty, I wanted to come talk to you sooner, but it wasn't safe."

Rosemary watched him out of the side of her eye. It wasn't very safe right now, which made her doubt the man.

"I knew Jack, and I liked him. I was ordered by Crane to meet up with Hector that night, kill him, and take the book."

"I'm gonna kill *you!*" Hector spat, pushing forward, but Rosemary stopped him with her gun.

"You little turncoat," Crane snarled at Frankie.

Frankie swallowed, dancing nervously in his spot. "I was just trying to protect Jack. Crane had thought all along that the book, which Jack had had with him that day in the mine, had been destroyed in the blast. But one of the men who helped with the recovery found it. It's a little burned but most of it's still intact. Hector obviously got it from that man. And now I have it. It doesn't belong to any of us."

"It belongs to me, you weasel," Crane said.

"Look, Mr. Crane, I know why you want it so badly. And it has nothing to do with the supposed doctoring of assay reports, which I'm not even certain that Jack was doing. You're worried about the other thing."

"What thing?" Shady Briggs asked.

"Crane was skimming profits from his mine," Frankie answered.

"Why would he do that?" Rosemary said. "It was his mine."

"He has silent partners. He was sending some of the gold in secret to an account in Salt Lake City. It was Jack who handled it for him, and he kept track of it in this book."

Rosemary's arms sagged a bit upon hearing of even more deceit by Jack, her limbs already aching from holding the gun for so long.

"You have no idea what you're talking about,"

Crane said to Frankie, "so you best keep your supposed accusations to yourself. And let's be clear on one thing—you're fired."

"Fine by me. I no longer want to work for a man like you."

"Mrs. Ben Wheeler," Shady Briggs interrupted in a snide voice. "I had no idea there was so much drama in this town. How about you put the gun down, and we'll all discuss this."

With her spirit and body succumbing to exhaustion, a part of Rosemary wished this would all go away.

In the waning light, she didn't see Shady reach for a gun hidden behind him in his trousers' waistband. He grabbed the nearest man to him—Mortimer Crane—and gripped his prisoner's neck with a hard yank of his arm, then pointed the weapon at Crane's head.

"You'll take me to McGinty," he said, "or I'll kill Crane."

Struggling to keep her own gun at the ready, she almost laughed at the wild panic in Crane's eyes. Hector and Alvin moved aside, and Rosemary didn't have the energy to keep them in place. In her gut, she knew they were the lesser evil. They moved to stand near her and Frankie, and they all watched Briggs inciting raw fear in Mortimer Crane.

She was ashamed by the sliver of satisfaction she felt from the display before her.

"You can kill him," Hector said. "I don't think any of us care."

"Well, I ain't no accessory to murder, so they'll not be any shootin'," Alvin complained. "I was promised a claim by this snake. It was the only reason I agreed to bring him here."

"Who's the turncoat now," Hector mumbled to his friend.

"All's fair in claims and gold," Alvin uttered back.

"What do you say, Crane?" Shady asked. "Should I kill you?"

"Please, no." Mortimer Crane whimpered like a baby.

Chapter Twenty

Rosemary held her breath in stunned silence as she waited for Shady Briggs to shoot Mortimer Crane in the head.

Frankie nudged her shoulder. "I have the book," he whispered. "You can have it. I brought it for you."

She twisted her neck and stared at the scrawny young man. "You have it *with* you?" She was unable to keep the shock from her lowered voice, inciting what happened next.

Hector lunged at Frankie, attacking him. "That's mine, you imbecile."

They fell to the ground. Alvin screamed and tried to intercede. Rosemary scrambled to step back before they dragged her into the ruckus. Raising her gaze back to Briggs, she saw the ruffian lying on the ground and Crane hightailing it toward the horses just beyond the tree line, his coat flapping behind him.

Rosemary sprang forward, determined to stop Crane before he reached Frankie's saddlebags. He was surely after the book. As she ran past Briggs, his hand caught her ankle and she slammed into the ground, rattling her teeth and knocking the air from her lungs.

"Oh no you don't," Briggs growled. "You're my best bet of getting McGinty."

She rolled to her back, kicking at him to release her, but he was tenacious. She screamed and swung the butt of her gun toward his face, eliciting a loud crack as metal connected with bone. He let her go. She shuffled back and scrambled to her feet.

Crane had reached a horse and was rifling through the gear. When he pulled a book free, he tossed the saddlebags aside. Moving fast, Rosemary rushed him and grabbed at the book. Crane grunted and fought her, but she had the element of surprise and quickly wrenched it from his grasp. It was a sorry-looking thing, smudged and partially burnt, the dried pages swollen from water damage.

She ran to Madge, ready to mount, but with all the commotion the animal startled, causing her to rear back and snap the branch holding her reins. She bolted.

Again? Criminy, Madge.

Looking around, she spied one of the other horses, and rushed toward it when her attention was snagged by movement in the shadow of the trees. Two men fought.

Was Hector still attacking Frankie? But with a sinking suspicion, she knew it wasn't them.

It was McGinty and Shady Briggs.

Her heart stopped. *Briggs will kill Miles.* Of that she had no doubt.

She pulled the gun from her coat pocket and bore down on the men.

"Get off him, Briggs!"

Briggs rolled McGinty beneath him, smashing Miles' face into the ground.

"Get out of here, Rosemary," Miles choked out.

She clasped both hands onto the gun and fired, knocking Briggs off Miles. McGinty immediately recovered and stood, yanking handcuffs from his coat and restraining the man.

Rosemary stood frozen. Once he'd taken care of Shady, Miles came to her.

"Are you all right?" He cupped the side of her face with his hand.

"Is he dead?" she whispered.

"Not yet. You hit him in the shoulder." He took the gun from her. "You saved me yet again."

"He wanted *you* dead."

"I'm glad to know you care." The intense longing in his gaze burned into her, then he turned away.

"Wait!" She grabbed his arm. "Don't do it."

"Do what?"

She looked down at her gun in his hand. "Kill him."

His face screwed with disgust and for a moment Rosemary didn't recognize the man she had lain beside these past days.

"Believe me," he said. "I want to. But I won't. Cordelia deputized me, so I'll arrest him. Then we need to get him to Doc Spense before he bleeds out."

"Where's Crane?" Rosemary blurted and spun around.

The horses were gone. Had they run off with Madge? More likely because of Madge. That horse was too boisterous when she got worked up.

Rosemary caught sight of Crane running away as fast as his chubby waddle would take him.

The book!

She had dropped it. Frantically, she scanned the ground around her, but it was obvious what had happened. Mortimer Crane had slithered in like the snake that he was and taken it while she'd been distracted by Miles fighting with Briggs.

"We need to go after Crane," Rosemary said. "He has the second ledger that Jack used. And it's worse than we thought. Crane was stealing from his own mine, and it's all in the book."

Miles whistled sharply, and his horse trotted forward. As Miles climbed on to the animal, smoke began to billow from Crane's position.

"Oh no!" Rosemary yelled, taking off at a run. "He's burning the evidence."

Miles covered the short distance quickly atop Pearl, but it was too late. The book was in flames. Suddenly, Madge burst from the trees, ran straight for Crane, and bit him soundly on the back of the neck. He fell to the ground, squealing like an injured animal.

Miles jumped off Pearl as she came to a stop, then pulled off his coat and threw it over the burning book. Rosemary halted when she reached them, out of breath. Miles lifted his coat and they both leaned over to inspect what remained. Unfortunately, it wasn't much.

Crane pushed to his feet, blood oozing between

his fingers as he tried to staunch the flow coming from his neck. "That horse needs to be shot."

"Over my dead body," Rosemary said, every word punctuated with anger. "Madge deserves a reward. Jack is dead because of you, because you sent him into the mine that day, because you made him do your dirty work. You're despicable, Crane."

"I'm what?" he sputtered, red soaking the white collar of his shirt. "You can't speak to me that way. And your husband was a criminal."

"It takes a criminal to know one, doesn't it?" she replied.

"You've got evidence of nothing," he countered.

She willed her temper into submission. "We should leave you out here with Briggs and let you both bleed to death." Her voice was surprisingly calm.

"It certainly has merit," Miles said. "But I aim to see Shady Briggs rot in jail for his crimes. As for you, Crane, it's only a matter of time."

Crane's breathing became labored as he struggled to unbutton the collar of his shirt, now soaked in blood. "For what?" he cried.

"To see your empire fall."

Chapter Twenty-one

September 14, 1884

Rosemary stepped out of church, still conflicted. Time spent in prayer hadn't yielded the answers she sought.

She paused and watched the townsfolk as they left the building, nodding at Buster and Thad, and Eleanora and her new husband, Reed, who carried a sleeping little Tessa in his arms.

Cora appeared at her side. "Is he here?"

Rosemary glanced at her friend. "Who?"

"Your husband."

Rosemary smoothed her hands down her dress. "No, and I don't expect to see him. He took Shady Briggs all the way to Salt Lake City."

"He'll return," Cora stated.

"I'm not so sure."

"Why? Because you told him you were done with the marriage?"

"Well … yes."

"Are you? Done with it?"

Rosemary had been certain that time apart would make her heart grow tepid toward Miles, but in fact a desperate longing had gripped her.

But how could she trust him? She had come to services this morning in search of inspiration, but she was just as confused now as ever.

She sighed. "I don't know."

Cora hooked her arm with Rosemary's. "Let's get over to the Crystal Café before Garnet sells out of everything to this hungry church crowd."

Rosemary had to walk quickly as Cora took off like a locomotive.

"You want to know what I think?" Cora asked. "You love him. More than you'd like to admit." They made a left on Elm Avenue, her words matching the staccato of her boots on the boardwalk.

Do I love Miles?

She had thought she loved Jack, but there had been so much he had kept from her. It was clear that the entire foundation of that love was shaky at best, and Rosemary could only conclude that the ability of her heart to guide her was flawed.

"If you end the marriage, how will you pay

McGinty back?" Cora asked.

She had the bullion she'd discovered, but she'd told no one of it. That was another source of uncertainty. What should she do with it?

She hadn't returned to the mine—The Floriana, as she thought of it now, whether it was the old mine or not—fearing that she could be followed once again, despite that Hector, Alvin and Frankie had all left the area, apparently fearing that staying near Mortimer Crane wasn't worth the trouble.

"That's a consideration," Rosemary admitted.

"Well, there's nothing like a little pie to solve our problems."

"For breakfast?"

Cora smiled. "We women of Wildcat Ridge cannot be contained by rules, can we?"

They made the turn on to Front Street, the soothing gurgle of Moose Creek greeting them.

Rosemary nodded her agreement, thinking of her uneasy truce with Crane.

While he had destroyed the second ledger that had held so much incriminating evidence against him, Rosemary had confessed everything to Cordelia nevertheless. And while the marshal had admitted that without any evidence, there was little she could do, she had put a whisper of retribution into Crane's ear.

The outcome was that Crane had agreed to leave Rosemary alone, and for now, she would take it. With Frankie Edwards gone, she had quite insistently told Crane that she would run the only assay office in these parts, and that he wouldn't stop business from coming to her.

She looked forward to her life finally returning to some semblance of normal.

As they neared the Crystal Café, Cora said, "I know you don't want to hear it, but forgiveness is good for the soul."

"Are you asking me to forgive you for departing soon to be with Charles and leaving me behind?"

They entered the café and Garnet waved at them from across the room, motioning them over to a table in front of the window.

Cora settled in her chair and removed her hat, then cast a compassionate look at Rosemary. "I know you've been let down by the men in your life, but you can't keep running away from them."

Cora's words struck a chord. When Miles returned, *if he returned*, Rosemary would need to decide—would she end the marriage, or would she stay?

Chapter Twenty-two

October 4, 1884

It was late afternoon, and the Harvest Festival was in full swing. Rosemary was glad that Hester hadn't canceled because of the chilly weather. Everyone in town needed a chance to relax and socialize, and Rosemary had been especially glad for the distraction.

She had spent the morning at the Ridge Hotel hovering over the pie competition. Since she had no idea how to bake a worthy dessert, she had instead brought her surplus of potatoes from her larder and happily gifted the vegetables to anyone who would have them.

After visiting with many of her friends at that event, she had headed to Tweedie's Mercantile to help distribute donated clothing to those in need. Now, she was huddled on the boardwalk on Front Street with a crowd of enthusiastic townsfolk, waiting for the three-legged race to begin.

Dulcina came to stand beside her.

"Is that Gabriel out there?" Rosemary asked, spying Dulcina's tall husband among the participants. He was paired up with one of the children in town.

Dulcina laughed, her dark eyes flashing. "He's quite enjoying himself. How are you?"

The simple question caused Rosemary to unravel, startling her with its intensity. Dulcina must have noticed because she put an arm around her and guided her toward the Last Chance Saloon, the establishment that she had run with her first husband, Stuart, and now ran with Gabriel.

It had been over two weeks, and Rosemary had heard nothing from Miles. With each day that had passed, she was forced to face the fact that he had indeed used her. Shady Briggs had come looking for Jack, and she had been nothing more than bait, a means to an end. Any endearment that Miles had whispered to her during the few days when they had lived as true man and wife were but fleeting sentiments. She had vacillated between anger and a deep sense of loss, and it had been difficult when Cora departed for Salt Lake City a week ago with

Charles. Rosemary had almost accompanied her, despite that she had plenty of assay jobs to keep her busy each day. She had been ready to go looking for Miles and give him a piece of her mind. *How dare he so blithely abandon their marriage!*

But in the end, she had decided she was better off not chasing the man. She was uncertain how to go about divorcing him, let alone deal with all the financial issues, but she resigned herself to speaking with Hester next week about it. Perhaps the attorney, Owen Vaile, who had helped Hester with the hot springs, could advise Rosemary.

Dulcina unlocked the door and let them both into the saloon. "Come inside and sit for a while," she said, guiding Rosemary to a table and handing her an embroidered kerchief.

Rosemary wiped at her eyes. "I'm fine." Embarrassed by her sudden display of emotion, she tried to compose herself.

Dulcina took a seat beside her. "We don't know each other well, but I did hear about what happened in the wilderness with you and your husband and Mortimer Crane. Has Miles told you when he will return?"

Rosemary cleared her throat. "No." She

hesitated. "I don't think he's coming back."

The saloon owner's dark eyes rounded. "Why would you say that?"

"Well, before he left, I had kicked him out."

"Why?"

"He lied to me. Jack lied to me." She rubbed her forehead. "I'm thinking I'm better off alone."

"Do you really believe that?"

Rosemary couldn't answer.

"Stuart and I didn't have a perfect marriage," Dulcina said, "and I most certainly didn't want to marry again, but it's difficult for a woman alone. At the beginning with Gabriel I feared I had made a mistake, but now …" She clasped her hands to her chest. "I can't imagine being without him."

"Yes, but didn't you know him long before you married him? You had a friendship to rely on, a history. Miles and I don't have that."

"But don't you see?" She shook her head and a wisp of dark hair loosened from her bun. "None of that matters. Something that is hard to explain occurred between me and Gabriel, and if you stop trying to reason your way through it, I think you'll find the same thing has happened between you and Miles."

Rosemary gave her a questioning look.

"The only sentiment that comes to mind," Dulcina said, her smile widening, "is bliss."

Rosemary froze. Miles had mentioned the very same word in what now felt like ages ago.

"I sometimes think …" Dulcina rested a hand on Rosemary's arm, "that giving oneself to another person doesn't diminish us, but rather makes us who we are meant to be. We become the best version of ourselves *because* of that person, not in spite of it."

The woman's gaze shifted to a point beyond Rosemary's shoulder. "Speaking of fate."

"I didn't think we were," Rosemary replied softly, wondering where this conversation had come from, but she felt close to Dulcina in a way she hadn't with any of the other women in town. Perhaps she understood more than the others what Rosemary had gone through.

Dulcina looked back at her and gave her knee a little nudge, nodding toward the doorway.

Rosemary turned and gasped, her heart pounding double time.

Miles stood at the entrance.

Chapter Twenty-three

Rosemary stood, anticipation flooding her. As Miles pulled off his hat, he watched her with a stark longing in his eyes, his appearance haggard and his cheeks reddened. From the cold? Or was he experiencing the same eagerness as her?

Dulcina stood. "I need to get back to the festival, so I'll just let you two have some privacy," she said and left.

"Did you just get here?" Rosemary asked.

Miles nodded. "I've been looking all over town for you."

She took a deep breath. "Why didn't you write? Or send a telegram? I've been worried sick."

"I'm sorry, but I didn't think … well, I wasn't sure if you'd want to hear from me. And I got back as soon as I could. Dealing with Briggs took longer than I thought. But your friend, Mrs. Drummond, contacted me a few days ago. She said …."

"She said what?"

"She said that maybe I ought to get home to my wife and fix my marriage. I won't lie. It gave me hope that maybe you didn't still want to throw me out."

She gripped the back of the chair with one hand to steady herself.

"I'm sorry I lied to you, Rosemary. I shouldn't have, but I was trying to protect you. And Jack. He should have told you the truth as well, but I suspect he was afraid you would leave him, just as I was."

"I know." She'd had much time to think on everything that had happened. "I went to the cemetery and made my peace with Jack. I also wrote a letter to my father, asking him if we could talk soon."

"Any chance you might extend that forgiveness to me?"

"Yes," she replied softly. "But I have something to tell you. I found what I believe to be The Floriana Mine. It's played out, but I discovered a bag of gold bullion."

"I know."

"You do? How?"

"I ran into Cordelia when I was out searching for

you and she filled me in. Why didn't you keep it? It would have allowed you to divorce me and be financially independent."

"That's true."

"Cordelia said you gave it to the authorities to make restitution for Jack's crimes."

She nodded. "When Jack and I first married, it's clear that he supported us with that money. The same money that Shady was demanding from me. It was the only thing I could do to make right what Jack had done."

"Most people would have kept such unexpected good fortune."

Rosemary smiled. "When Crane heard, he tried to slap a lawsuit on me, stating that I'd overlapped on claims he owned. Hester's attorney looked at it and there was no merit to it."

"How's the wound Madge gave him?"

She laughed. "Festering."

"Serves him right."

Miles came to stand before her.

"So it would seem that I can't pay you back just yet," Rosemary said softly.

"You don't *ever* have to pay me back."

"What do you want in return?"

He reached a hand to her cheek and lightly cupped it. "Stay with me and be my wife."

She stepped closer to him. "I may consider it," she teased. "On one condition."

"You must know that I'd do anything for you."

"Stop attacking men in the woods. First Hector, then Shady Briggs. I don't much care for seeing you pinned to the ground while your face turns a dark shade of purple."

He pulled her into his arms. "But twice you saved me."

"You know I'd do anything for you, but I'm hanging up my gun. Or maybe I should ask Cordelia for a job?"

"No. Please stick to assays. And I'll stick with carpentry. I was thinking of talking to George Tweedie about the possibility of opening a sawmill in town."

"Oh, Miles," she exclaimed, filled with hope for the future. "That would be a tremendous boon for the town."

"These past few weeks, all I could think about was how much I want to build a future with you. And we'll do it together in Wildcat Ridge. It's the best possible way I can think of to honor the lives of all the men who were lost in the mine accident. A way to honor Jack."

"Johnny," she added.

"I think he would prefer we remember him as Jack."

"I'll always miss him."

"I know. I would never ask you to forget the life you had with him. I love you, Rosemary."

Tears filled her eyes. "I love you, too."

Holding her close, he tenderly kissed her, and there was only one word to describe how she felt.

Bliss.

THE END

If you enjoyed *Rosemary*, would you consider posting a review? Not only does this help other readers discover a story, but it also aids an author in pursuing promotional opportunities. My heartfelt thanks. ~ Kristy

About the Author

Kristy McCaffrey writes historical western romances brimming with grit and emotion, along with contemporary adventure stories packed with smoldering romance and spine-tingling suspense. Her work is filled with compelling heroes, determined heroines, and her trademark mysticism. Kristy holds a bachelor's and master's degree in mechanical engineering, but writing has been her passion since she was very young. Her four children are nearly grown and gone, so she and her husband frequently pursue their love of travel to the far corners of the world. Kristy believes life should be lived with curiosity, compassion, and gratitude, and one should never be far from the enthusiasm of a dog. An Arizona native, she resides in the desert north of Phoenix. To learn more about her work, visit Kristy's website or sign up for her newsletter to receive her latest book news as well as subscriber-only content. She also posts pics of her travels and dogs at Instagram.

Visit Kristy on Social Media

Website
    https://kmccaffrey.com/

Newsletter:
        https://kmccaffrey.com/subscribe/

Facebook:
    https://www.facebook.com/AuthorKristyMcCaffrey/

Twitter:
        https://www.twitter.com/McCaffreyKristy/

Instagram:
        https://www.instagram.com/kristymccaffrey/

The Widows of Wildcat Ridge

A Sweet Historical Western Romance Series
Don't miss all the great stories!

Find all the books at our Amazon Series Page—
https://amzn.to/2RJaCX3

www.ingramcontent.com/pod-product-compliance
Lightning Source LLC
Chambersburg PA
CBHW050734230626
47052CB00002BA/190